SILENCED: REFUSED TO BE SILENCED

Inspired by A True Story

ALBERT & AIMEE ANDERSON

authorHOUSE®

AuthorHouse™
1663 Liberty Drive
Bloomington, IN 47403
www.authorhouse.com
Phone: 833-262-8899

This is a work of fiction. All of the characters, names, incidents, organizations, and dialogue in this novel are either the products of the author's imagination or are used fictitiously.

Published by AuthorHouse 01/31/2023

ISBN: 978-1-6655-7974-2 (sc)
ISBN: 978-1-6655-7975-9 (hc)
ISBN: 978-1-6655-7973-5 (e)

Library of Congress Control Number: 2023900349

Print information available on the last page.

Any people depicted in stock imagery provided by Getty Images are models, and such images are being used for illustrative purposes only. Certain stock imagery © Getty Images.

Fictionalized story.
Inspired by a true story.

This book is printed on acid-free paper.

In memory of my dear husband:

Albert Emmanuel Anderson

We dedicate this book to our wonderful Heavenly Father who has always been and is so faithful and gracious to us.

To all our precious children, grandchildren, and great-grandchildren.

To all of God's dear children, His sheep, who have been wrongfully wounded by the "shepherds" of the flock.

No one can control all the circumstances and events that come to us day by day. Oftentimes things happen over which we have no control. However, each one of us *can* control our *reaction* to what transpires in our lives. We can make a conscious choice whether we will allow the events of our lives to make us *bitter* or *better*. We can become bitter as acid—mean, sour, miserable to be with or near—or we can use (with God's grace and help) the happenings of our lives to make us more loving, kind, considerate of others—more like Jesus!

Bless the Lord, O my soul: and all that is within me, bless his holy name. Bless the Lord, O my soul, and forget not all his benefits: Who forgiveth all thine iniquities; who healeth all thy diseases.

—Psalm 103:1–3)

If we say that we have no sin, we deceive ourselves, and the truth is not in us. If we confess our sins, he is faithful and just to forgive us our sins, and to cleanse us from all unrighteousness.

—1 John 1:8–9)

ACKNOWLEDGMENTS

I express my profound appreciation and thanks to my daughter, Deborah Anderson Chase, for her loving and gracious foreword.

I wish to express my profound appreciation and thanks to Larissa Chase Budreau, my granddaughter (Deborah and Larry's daughter) for designing the beautiful cover of this book.

Most of all with great thankfulness I acknowledge the profound and eternal truths from the inspired Word of God, the Holy Bible. The main source of scripture quotations used in this book is the King James Version of the Bible.

SPECIAL THANKS

To our wonderful Heavenly Father: for His faithful, loving, patient, and persistent dealings in our lives to make us more like Him. In addition, we give our Lord a special great big heartfelt thanks for the Holy Word of God, and the eternal and everlasting principles of faith, hope, and love contained therein that daily inspire and guide us in paths of righteousness.

To my parents, Olaus and Minnie Filan (Aimee's deceased father and mother) and Albert and Hazel Anderson (Albert's deceased father and mother). We are grateful to the Lord for the godly influence our parents exerted on us. We consider ourselves blessed and enriched. We are thankful for our heritage, knowing our parents are "at home" with the Lord.

To my precious, beautiful children, grandchildren, and great-grandchildren. My heart is full to overflowing with love for *all* our precious children, grandchildren, great-grandchildren, and soon great-great-grandchildren. I am so thrilled and delighted to receive these beautiful gifts of love straight from Heaven. God daily reminds me that *He is still with me/us.* All, of my children, grandchildren, and great-grandchildren continue to thrill and delight me with their love and beauty. I daily name them all off to God in prayer, asking our wonderful Father in Heaven to watch over each of my children, asking Him to please keep all of them safe in His care and love. My heart is big enough to love and cherish as many children and grandchildren as God gives to me. I love it! Thank you, Lord God of Heaven and Earth, for my precious family.

Finally, I wish to express my deep heartfelt thanks and gratefulness to and for my dear, precious (deceased 3/9/13) husband, Albert, for the constant inspiration, encouragement, earnest prayers, loyalty, faithfulness, and devoted love we received from each other as husband and wife for (almost fifty-nine awesome years) fifty-eight years and eleven months to the day. I have always been very grateful and thankful to the Lord for giving me this earthly treasure—a godly husband. And I wish to thank Albert (now in Heaven) for his wonderful gospel messages that he daily lived and preached, as well as for his beautiful and very sweet love letters written to me, and for our awesome, amazing love that we shared through the many years.

Blessed is the man that walketh not in the counsel of the ungodly, nor standeth in the way of sinners, nor sitteth in the seat of the scornful. But his delight is in the law of the Lord; and in his law doth he meditate day and night. And he shall be like a tree planted by the rivers of water, that bringeth forth his fruit in his season; his leaf also shall not wither; and whatsoever he doeth shall prosper.

—Psalms 1:1–3

FOREWORD

So many times in life we can miss precious opportunities to help those in need as Jesus would have us do. My parents, Albert and Aimee Anderson, just happened to be "those" individuals who adhered to the gospel message totally and completely. When people came for help, they would minister to and pray with those individuals, and then they would do all they could to help in that situation. *Never* did they ever say, "We want to expose corruption." Never did they say, "That person has done wrong; we need to correct them!" That was *never* their intention. So when multiple people in any given circumstance came to them for help because they had been persecuted or wrongly accused, my dad and mom in their absolute devotion and submission to Jesus and his Word could not turn down a plea for help! Had they known what was going to transpire by helping these individuals, I really believe that they would have still helped all these people, because that is what Jesus would have done; and my parents lived a life devoted to Jesus. *Even* when you were "persecuted for righteousness' sake" your promise was "for theirs is the kingdom of Heaven!" (Matthew 5:10); they never backed down from their biblical beliefs and values to live and act like Jesus! We are to be like Jesus—*no matter what!* So I just want to say thank you to my parents, Albert Emmanuel and Aimee Donalda Filan Anderson, for *never* compromising the gospel of Jesus. You always strived to spread the gospel and be the hands and feet of Jesus—always ministering to all those in need! That was your life, and I for one am so grateful for how your faith and devotion to Jesus consistently played out in your daily lives!

—Deborah Anderson Chase

This world is on the edge of moral decay. America's strength cannot rise above the righteousness and strength of her churches. Faithless and false leadership in the church leads to spiritual devastation and ruin not only for the leaders but for the people they lead. Many times people are balanced precariously between heaven and hell; thus, the truth must not be altered, watered down, or compromised, whether it be in the church or in the US government.

CHAPTER 1

Pastor Prince and Princess were enjoying their quiet evening together. They were still savoring a most delicious dinner.

"Well, sweetheart, that was an absolutely scrumptious meal."

"Thank you, dear. You are so easy to cook for. Oh, oh! I think someone is coming to see us."

Ella Church and the parsonage home took up most of the block. A new Cadillac pulled up in front of the parsonage. A sharp-looking man in a suit and tie stepped out of the car and walked up the sidewalk to ring the front doorbell.

"Oh, good evening, Rocky. Please come right in." Prince reached out his hand with a friendly handshake and a big smile.

"Hi! Rocky! Welcome to our home," Princess warmly greeted Rocky. "How are you?"

"Oh, I'm doing fine," Rocky responded with an outstretched handshake and sat down on the couch that Prince had so graciously offered him. Rocky looked around the beautiful living room, puffed out his chest, and began his prepared speech. "Prince, I am sure you are well aware that you and your wife, Princess, have a beautiful church and beautiful parsonage; you are very fortunate. You have pastored here at least ten years now, haven't you?"

"Yes, we have, and my wife and I love it; we love the people, and they love us. We are grateful and thankful for this place of ministry. We love living here very much and enjoy pastoring our church flock. They take good care of us."

"Good! I just hope my unexpected visit to your comfortable home is not going to interrupt any of your plans," Rocky continued with his pompous speech.

"Oh, no; my wife and I were just sitting here relaxing, enjoying the wonderful evening. The weather has been really great the last few days. What brings you to our fair city?"

"After our phone conversation the other day, I thought it would be good to visit you and your wife in your home."

"My wife and I consider it an honor to have the financial chairman of the Northwest District, the pastor of Bethel, and the president and the pastor of the Ranch Ministry come to visit us."

"Thank you. Hopefully, I can answer your questions in person and quiet any concerns you have concerning the District Rehabilitation Home Missions Project at Kitty, which is located so close to you, almost here in your backyard. I understand that Ryon and Jane Shin have occasionally attended your church."

"Yes, they have. And we do have a few questions we would like some answers to. Ryon and Jane, your Caring counselors, recently attended our Sunday morning service for the first time. We welcomed them to our community and told them we would be pleased to have them attend our church anytime."

"Ryon told me that he visited you in your church."

"Yes, they do occasionally come to our services. He told me that they will attend our church as much as possible, although they are committed to attending your church, even though it is difficult because your church is located clear across the state from us. Later, Ryon told us you ordered him to attend Pastor Jay's church in Kitty, instead of my church when, for some special reason, he cannot make the trip to your church." Prince hesitated, then decided he must continue sharing his thoughts with Pastor Rocky. "It sounds like Ryon has two pastors, you and Pastor Jay, and has no choice of where he attends church. Is this true?"

"Yes and no. Ryon works with Ray Beade, the ranch director for the Caring Outreach Ministry, and also for me. Ray and Visha Beade, and Ryon and Jane, the counselors, do have two pastors—Pastor Jay at Kitty Church, and I am their Caring pastor." Rocky swelled with his importance.

"I see!" Pastor Prince quietly answered as he looked directly into Rocky's shifty eyes.

"The first Sunday morning they came to our church, Jane gave me a Caring brochure that stated, 'Beade's ministry involves developing therapy projects, livestock and crop planning, and involvement in residents' spiritual/physical growth.' Ryon and Jane have now become our friends. Rocky, I think you need to know that Jane and I became friends the first time we met. It now is more than your church or Prince's church. Jane and I have become close friends," declared Princess.

"She told us that you hired both her and her husband to work at the ranch in counseling and schedule coordination to minister to the residents in the area of food service, schedule planning, spiritual/physical growth, prayer, and counseling," Prince said.

"It's a little complicated," Rocky responded with concern. "In addition, Ray is also the board member of Kitty, and his wife, Visha, is the church treasurer. Ray and his wife have several adopted children, which complicates things all the more."

"That is very interesting." Princess noticed that Rocky acted nervous, like something was bothering him.

"Rocky, how do you pay the Shins?" asked Prince.

"My wife and I talked it over and decided to give Ryon a gift of $200 a week," Rocky replied.

Princess felt compelled to ask another pressing question. "Jane told us that each week her husband, Ryon, makes a copy of two $100 bills on a sheet of paper, which you have requested Ryon to sign for you to use as a receipt for that week's services. We understand it is for your church records. Is this correct?"

Rocky tried to give a convincing answer. "My wife and I prayed about it and agreed to give a personal contribution to Ryon out of our own money."

Prince followed his wife's question with another accusing question. "Rocky, are you reimbursed by the insurance company for the weekly $200 salary you pay or give as a personal gift from you and your wife to Ryon for his ranch work? Yet, at the same time, your Caring Ranch Ministry brochure requests contributions from the churches and individuals to pay the staff salaries."

The atmosphere was becoming tense, and in defense, Rocky answered, "I told the insurance company all about it, and they said it was OK."

Princess continued questioning Rocky's integrity. "Did you tell Ryon not to tell the insurance company about the $200 cash receipts that you received from him?"

Rocky knew his life was on the line as he answered Princess in self-defense, "No! Do you believe me?"

Princess quickly responded, "I'm trying!"

Prince was shocked at his wife's response to Rocky's question but carried on with another very pointed, accusing statement and question of his own. "We were also told that you inflated the hay hauling freight bill and collected from the insurance company. Is that correct?"

Rocky became cocky in self-defense as he answered, "Whatever I do with the insurance company has been approved by the insurance company."

Without hesitation, Princess continued with another very incriminating question. "Rocky, do you have any of your personal cattle out at the Caring Ranch?"

"Oh—ah. No!"

"Really?" Princess softly responded.

Rocky's face turned white with guilt as he slowly answered, "Well, ah, maybe I have one or my son has one or two—or possibly more. I think it is time for me to go. I hope I have settled all your concerns."

With stooped shoulders, Rocky stood up and walked to the door to leave. The balloon of his deceitful self-inflated importance had been severely pierced with the truth.

Prince and Princess followed Rocky to the door where, again, Pastor Prince pleaded with him for integrity. "Rocky, I don't want your Ranch Ministry to be doing or be involved in anything that would be questionable or be a reproach to the gospel."

Rocky did not respond to Prince's request, but he stopped at the door, put his arm around Pastor Prince's shoulder, patted him on the back, and talked to him in a very chummy manner.

"We're buddies! Remember?"

After the goodbyes, Prince and Princess sat down on the couch and talked.

"Oh, honey, do you realize that we are involved in a big mess because we have befriended Ryon and Jane Shin by coming to their defense? In so doing, we are questioning the district officials' activities."

"I know. Isn't it terrible? I believe Rocky was very dishonest with us tonight. Don't you think so?"

"Yes! It appears to me that something is really troubling Rocky. Why would he take the time to make a special visit to our home?"

"Sounds to me like Jane's concerns about Rocky and the Kitty Ranch Ministry's lack of integrity are valid."

"I agree. You know, honey, you gave me quite a surprise tonight; I didn't know what to think when you answered Rocky's devious question the way you did. Rocky appeals to you to believe him with his very deceptive question, and you saying, 'I am trying!' was amazing to me but was shocking to Rocky's self-importance."

"I didn't believe him, but I was trying to believe him. I guess I spoke what I was thinking. I hope my answer was OK; I wanted to be honest."

"I think you gave him a fabulous answer. I am proud of you, sweetheart. You are a woman of character and a very loyal and devoted wife."

"Thank you, honey."

"Let's just forget Rocky and his ministry for the night and go to bed. But first I want a big hug and kiss from my one and only sweetheart."

Still sitting on the couch, Prince drew Princess into his arms in a very warm, tender, and loving embrace. He gently kissed her several times.

Princess responded by snuggling deeper into her husband's loving arms.

"Thank you, sweetheart. Thank you for your tender love and care for me all these many years. You are such a wonderful lover, husband, father, grandfather, pastor, preacher, teacher, and man of God. I love you more than ever."

"I know that God is still with us, has always been faithful to us, and He will see us through anything to glorious triumphant victory."

"I agree. But sometimes things get very complicated and difficult."

"That is right, my darling. Now let's forget everything else and go to bed for the night. Besides, I would much rather think about you, my sweet love; you are so beautiful!"

Prince reached for both of Princess' hands and pulled her up from the couch. They walked to their bedroom holding hands. The events of the troubling evening were forgotten as once again they became overwhelmed with their tender and precious love for each other.

> No weapon that is formed against thee shall prosper; and every tongue that shall rise against thee in judgment thou shalt condemn. This is the heritage of the servants of the Lord, and their righteousness is of me, saith the Lord. (Isaiah 54:17)

> Beloved, think it not strange concerning the fiery trial which is to try you, as though some strange thing happened unto you: But rejoice, inasmuch as ye are partakers of Christ sufferings; that, when his glory shall be revealed, ye may be glad also with exceeding joy. (1 Peter 4:12–13)

> Weeping may endure for a night, but joy cometh in the morning. (Psalm 30:5)

CHAPTER 2

Justin, a church board member, with a weed sprayer on his back, was spraying the weeds on the Kitty church property. Pastor Jay called out the parsonage door. "Justin, could I speak to you for a few minutes? Will you come here?"

"Oh, hello, Pastor," Justin responded as he took off the weed sprayer and walked over to the open back door. He stepped into the kitchen and leaned against the kitchen counter.

Pastor Jay was quick to reveal his reason for wanting Justin's attention. "Justin, why didn't you come with your wife to last night's counseling session?"

"Pastor, I didn't ask to be counseled by anyone. You told my wife and me to come to your office a few weeks ago, because you told me that you wanted to talk to us about something really important."

"That's right, it is important."

"I didn't have any idea you would call it a marriage counseling session and that you would schedule regular counseling sessions for my wife and me without our desire or request."

"You are not to question us, Justin. God leads us. We have been sent to this church on a mission. God has shown me that you and your wife need counseling."

"I do not agree with you, Pastor. I was proud of my wife, Patsy, for standing up to you and telling you she loves me, and she told you that she would not come to any more of your counseling sessions."

Pastor Jay's wife suddenly spoke up, "Justin, my husband and I are your pastors, and you have to submit to us."

"I am sorry, Mrs. Jay, I do not feel that way. If my wife wants to continue, that's up to her. I have had enough; I do not need counseling. I think my wife has had enough too."

"You are in rebellion! You must submit to my authority," declared Pastor Jay.

"Pastor, I know a lot of people are afraid to tell you why they have stopped coming to church."

"A lot of people in this church need to submit to their pastor's God-given authority." Pastor Jay swelled with his self-inflated power.

"Little by little stories are beginning to leak out about the guilt trips, intimidation, and confidences being used against them in front of the whole group. They are told to swear to keep secret the things *'God reveals'* to them in meetings, and fear of what the pastor's wife will do if they ever tell anyone what is going on."

"Justin, things are going to get very tough around here if people do not submit to their pastor's God-given authority."

"Things are being whispered about my wife and me being counseled by you. I have had enough of your counseling sessions. If my wife wants to continue, that's up to her. Pastor, one of your sessions is enough for me."

"God has told me that you need help. You need to submit to your pastor and come to your scheduled counseling sessions."

"Not me! I am through. Thanks anyway. Goodbye."

That same evening Pastor Jay phoned Patsy and talked her into attending one more counseling session without her husband.

When Patsy arrived for her counseling, Pastor Jay was quick to reveal his purpose. "Patsy, when you file for divorce, I want you to come to us, and we will help you."

"Pastor, what are you saying? I am never going to divorce my husband! I love him very much. I agree with my husband. I am through with your counseling too. Goodbye."

Sunday evening, church choir members were gathered for their weekly choir practice. Pastor Jay walked into the room to start the meeting with prayer.

"Anyone have a prayer request?"

"Pastor, please pray for my healing, and pray for Rita. She has been seriously ill for several months. In fact, she was in the emergency room of the hospital last night for six hours. I, also, need prayer because I have not been feeling well." Wendy continued with her plea for prayer and help. "That is why I have been absent from choir practice for the last three weeks—I have been very ill."

"Well, nobody knew about Rita."

Janet echoed the pastor. "Nobody knew about it."

Wendy could hardly believe what she was hearing. "I'm confused about what constitutes an emergency. The original prayer chain has been disbanded, and there are only five left. We have been told not to call unless it is a dire emergency."

The choir members began gathering around Rita and Wendy to pray for them.

With great disapproval written on his face, Pastor Jay suddenly stepped in front of Wendy. He spoke to Wendy in an angry tone. "Wendy, come with me to my office."

Wendy picked up her purse and Bible and followed Pastor Jay to his church office, when suddenly he started talking over his shoulder.

"Wendy, you sound like you have a bee in your bonnet."

"I suppose I do, Pastor."

They walked into the office. Pastor Jay turned and confronted Wendy.

"What's your problem?"

"Pastor, you took the prayer chain away, and you don't visit the sick. Poor Rita, nobody's visiting her except me and Ann. You never come to visit me unless I have a dinner."

"Whose problem is that?"

"Your problem, Pastor."

"Since you're so unhappy, find another church."

Pastor Jay pointed his finger to the door.

"With her head held high and shoulders erect, Wendy marched out of Pastor Jay's office without prayer. She was very disturbed. She drove to her mother's home to tell her what had transpired at choir practice.

"Mom, you will never believe what happened at choir practice. I have been kicked out of the church! What is going on with our pastor?"

"This is just a misunderstanding. The pastor is too young. Wendy, this will blow over; he did not mean it."

"No! Mom, it won't blow over."

Three days later, June 9, at 6:00 p.m., Pastor Jay phoned Wendy's mother, Patricia.

"Hello."

"Patricia, this is Pastor Jay. I want you to know that you are required to attend tomorrow night's board meeting!"

"Why? What is this all about?"

"You don't need to know. You just be there!"

"I will not come unless you tell me what this is all about!"

"You have aligned yourself with an evil spirit and have slandered everyone in the church."

"That is not true!"

"Woman, you have been living under a lying delusion for years."

"Pastor, please come and talk to me. I'll go before the church."

"No, you'll come before the board. Do you know what this means?"

"No, I don't know."

"If you do not submit and come before the board and let us deliver you of this evil spirit, it means you will never be allowed to step your foot inside this church again."

"Pastor, you can't do this."

"Don't ever let me see you step inside this church again."

Patricia hung up the phone and immediately phoned her daughter.

"Wendy, now I understand what you were trying to tell me about our pastor."

"Oh, Mom, I am so sorry! Mom, what is going on? Oh, I don't understand—I just don't get it!"

Later, Pastor phoned Wendy.

"Hello."

"I am calling to inform you that you are required to come to the church board meeting tonight."

Wendy was prepared for this phone call and quickly answered, "I don't think so! Not after what you said yesterday to my seventy-two-year-old mom."

"That is too bad; you are aligning yourself with an evil spirit."

"Pastor, I don't think so!"

Wendy promptly hung up the phone with a bang. She collapsed into a chair in utter shock. Her thoughts were all in a whirl—going back to about four or five weeks before when her pastor had praised her from the pulpit for her hospitality and commended her mother, Patricia, for having the gift of evangelism. Only a few weeks before, Pastor Jay had been at Wendy's home for banana splits. Now he had turned against her and her mother. Wendy was extremely angry at Pastor Jay for attacking her mother. She phoned her mom and her friends, Eve, Ann, Justin, and Patsy. She discussed the church service when Pastor Jay commended her mother publicly for her evangelistic gift, and the time when a group of church friends, including Pastor Jay, spent an evening in her home eating banana splits and having a good time of fellowship.

At the next church board meeting, June 10, Pastor Jay read the scripture, then, puffed out his chest as he unloaded on the church board.

"God has spoken to me. God has told me that because Patricia will not submit to her pastor and come to the board for us to pray for her and cast the evil spirit out of her, God will kill her. Her heart will just stop."

Justin, a board member, jumped up in defense of his friend, "I am out of here if this is what is going on. I resign."

Justin drove home very upset, crying and praying.

Patsy was sitting in her living room talking to her sister who was visiting from out of town when Justin came into the house. Patsy knew something was wrong by the look on her husband's face.

"What is wrong?"

"It's awful; I can't talk about it."

Justin walked into the bedroom. Patsy, who was very concerned, followed her husband into the bedroom. Justin sat down on the edge of the bed crying. Patsy put her loving arms around her husband.

11

"What happened?"

"I can't talk about it. It is so awful."

Patsy walked back into the living room and phoned one of the other board members.

"Jon, what happened at the board meeting? Justin is so upset he is crying and won't tell me what happened."

"Patsy, my stomach is in knots, and I can't talk about it either. You had better call Pastor."

Patsy decided to wait until morning because it was too late to make the call.

Early in the morning, Pastor Jay phoned Patsy.

"Hello. Patsy, I want to talk to you about last night's board meeting."

"Yes, I want to know what happened."

"Get your Bible. I want you to read with me some scripture that I read to the board last night regarding the issue of Patricia and Wendy."

Patsy followed along with her Bible and then asked her pastor, "Pastor Jay, what was Justin so upset about? He told me something happened at the end of the meeting, but he could not tell me what took place that so greatly disturbed him to the point of tears."

"Just a minute. I'll get to that after I read a few more scriptures to you."

Pastor finished reading the scriptures.

"What was Justin so upset about?"

"Well, God has revealed to me that if Patricia doesn't repent and come before the board and me, she is going to die."

"Pastor, wait a minute. I believe God's scriptures, but you're just a man, and you say God told you Patricia is going to die? I know other pastors who have been in the wrong, two of them. Pastor, I only go by God's Word."

"Well, it's good you feel that way, but I'm just warning you so when it happens, you won't be shocked. Patricia is going to die; her heart is just going to stop—not a heart attack—God is just going to kill her."

CHAPTER 3

Woe be unto the pastors that destroy and scatter the
sheep of my pasture! saith the Lord. Therefore thus
saith the Lord God of Israel against the pastors that
feed my people; Ye have scattered my flock, and
driven them away, and have not visited them: behold,
I will visit upon you the evil of your doings, saith the
Lord. And I will set up shepherds over them which
shall feed them: and they shall fear no more, nor be
dismayed, neither shall they be lacking, saith the Lord.
                                                —Jeremiah 23:1–2, 4

Soon into Pastor Jay's Sunday morning pastoral message, his true
dictatorial/control problem was revealed to the congregation. He was
not there to feed the flock of God. Apparently, his true purpose was to
shear the sheep. If he cut more than wool, and, cut deep into flesh as
well, that was just fine with him. He was out for blood as he verbally
attacked Patricia and her daughter.

"The sin in the Corinthian church—a son having sex with
his father's wife—is an example of needed church discipline.
Disciplinary action in the church is for the purpose of bringing
people to repentance, forgiveness, and restoration to the fellowship
of Christians. Immoral sin has to be dealt with and punished.

"An elderly widow, Patricia, and her daughter, Wendy, will no
longer be attending this church. The board has met and requested that
these two women appear before them to face charges of habitual lying
and gossip. They refuse to meet with the board; thus, the board has

agreed that the two women should no longer be allowed to worship with us in this church. It was not an option but a condition that they had to come before the pastor and the board, and they refused our request.

"The bottom line is Patricia and Wendy will not be coming back to this church. They have been expelled from the church, and no one from this congregation should have anything to do with them until they come to their pastor and board in true repentance."

Justin, a long-standing board member, jumped to his feet to defend his friends!

"We were not all in agreement with the action that was taken at the board meeting."

Deale was quick to jump to his feet and join Justin in defending their friends. "I know these two women; they are God fearing and good Christians. What have they done wrong?"

Two girls, Eve and Kate, began crying, so their mother, Deb, stood up to defend their friends.

"Why? What have they done?"

People were shouting, "What have they done," and all over the church you could hear people crying, "Why?" "Why?"

Pastor Jay wanted to show his power and authority, and to do so, he immediately had to take charge.

"I have ten things stored in my computer! And I can't tell you what they are because it would be gossip," said the pompous pastor before he quickly exited the church, thus escaping the angry crowd.

Later that evening Wendy and her mother were visiting together. They had been home about fifteen minutes when people started arriving at their door. Excitedly, they all wanted to share their story. Each one, in turn, told his or her version of what happened in the Sunday service.

Bea was quick to express her concerns. "What has happened to our young and enthusiastic pastor and wife? Pastor and Mrs. Jay came with a vision for church growth and a dynamic youth outreach. They seemed to be just what our quiet country church needed. Now look at the situation created by Pastor Jay's expulsion of our friends

Patricia and Wendy. It is so cruel and unjust to falsely accuse them and especially from the pulpit."

Patricia still felt the sting of Pastor Jay's cruel and false accusations against her as she spoke from her heart. "For months Pastor and his wife have been working their way into this church's favor—working toward total control of everyone."

"Yes," said Bea, "the youth group has grown and the teens, those who have been unruly, have been brought into submission. A drama team was started, and several well-done skits and plays were performed, both at the home church and in neighboring towns. New people began attending services and members were added, swelling the congregation."

Tears gathered in Patricia's eyes as she spoke from her heart. "Pastor Jay and his wife have won the people's love. In the beginning, we believed he was a true man of God. But over the last few months, I have observed some things which are very questionable."

Bea nodded in agreement, "Now there is a widening split that has developed in what was once a loving united fellowship of believers."

Patsy was overwhelmed with love and compassion for her friends who were suffering; her emotions almost got the best of her as she shared what she had witnessed that very morning.

"Some of us have known Patricia and Wendy for many years, and we feel sick about what has taken place. When we ask the pastor to tell us what these women have done, he falsely accuses them of being habitual slanderers and gossips. Then, in a Sunday morning church service, he inferred they were lesbians, followed by a command to all the church people not to have any dealings with them until there is repentance and asking of forgiveness." Patsy's eyes filled with tears as she spoke.

"How can we repent and ask forgiveness for something we have not done?"

Wendy was quick to defend her mother. "Pastor Jay needs to repent and ask forgiveness for publicly falsely accusing Mom and me and falsely inferring that we are lesbians."

Patsy wanted to help her friends but felt so helpless. "Now, everyone who questions Pastor Jay receives a letter telling them to leave the church because they are not in harmony with him."

"That's right! Pastor Jay is working toward total control of everyone who attends our church and getting rid of the old guard that has been here for years. It is becoming a cult!" Wendy was almost breathless with distress.

Patricia continued telling her tragic story. "After two-and-one half months of silence, I wrote a letter to Pastor Jay telling my side of what transpired. He has never told me what my *crime* is. He has never come to me as Matthew 18:15–17 admonishes, even though he falsely accused me of having a lying spirit and has repeatedly said I need deliverance. But I don't know what from! He is the one that has the lying spirit."

Ann, another of Patricia and Wendy's dear friends, could remain silent no longer. "Patricia, only a few months ago, Pastor Jay praised you from the pulpit for your evangelism."

"I feel a great injustice has taken place," said Casidy, "and we need to petition the local district to send someone to help settle this matter."

"Patricia, I hate to be the one to tell you that Pastor Jay is going around telling different people that you are going to die—that you are going to just drop dead. We did not want to tell you before but finally decided you needed to know what Pastor Jay is saying," said Ann.

"We certainly do have a lot to think and pray about," said Wendy.

"Thank you for warning us," declared Patricia. "I will be praying more than ever. Please join me in prayer as we all need God's protection."

"Patricia, you know that we will do what we can to defend you and Wendy," declared Justin.

Wendy shut down her day care for a few days and took her mom out of town.

"It is the first anniversary of Daddy's death. We are going to celebrate your fifty-three years, and besides, we need to get out of this town for a breath of fresh air."

"Thank you, Wendy; I do need to leave here for a few days. It is now 8:00 a.m. Let's do a lot of praying and singing of hymns, and God will help us understand what is taking place in our church and in our personal lives."

Wendy and Patricia really did not know where they were going. They ate breakfast at Snoqualmie Pass, walked around, drove on, and stopped at a motel in Elmont, ate dinner, and turned in for the night.

The next morning, while having a continental breakfast, they discussed their situation. "Wendy, I know what we are to do! We need to find Mindy."

"Who is Mindy? Mom, if you feel that you must find her, with God's help I will move heaven and earth to help you find Mindy. OK, let's go."

"I want to look at this map. I think she and her family have a nursery here in Elmont."

"Mom, is this the couple that you and Dad met at the last Elly Rodeo before Dad died?"

"Yes. Dad and I really liked them and their children. They told me that they own a nursery in Elmont. Let's stop at this old-fashioned hardware store. You stay in the car with your dog, and I will go in and ask for directions."

When the clerk handed Patricia a phone book, she leafed through the pages searching for the nursery number.

When she had found it, Patricia asked, "Will you dial that number for me?"

The clerk made the call and handed the phone to Patricia.

"Who is this?" Patricia asked.

"Mindy."

"Oh, it is so good to hear your voice, Mindy; this is Patricia."

"Patricia, where are you? We were just sitting here praying for you. About two weeks ago the Lord laid you on our hearts to pray for you; we just now finished praying for you during our devotions."

"Thank you. We need that. Just a minute, let me go get my daughter, Wendy, so you can give her instructions on how to find your home or place of business."

After receiving instructions, Wendy and Patricia drove about one and a half miles farther, and in a few minutes arrived at Mindy's nursery. After a time of fellowship and tea served by Mindy, Sam, Mindy's husband, said good-bye to the ladies and hurried back to work.

Patricia and Wendy told Mindy about their pastor forbidding them to come back to church. They talked on this subject for about thirty minutes. All this time they heard customers coming in and going out of their place of business. A bell would ring in their home every time someone came.

"Patricia, my husband needs to hear your story. Let's go talk to Sam."

One customer was in the store. Up until that time, the business bell rang at least twenty times, which indicated customers were coming in. When the last customer left, no more came in for over one hour. Patricia started telling her story to Sam. While Patricia was telling her story, Sam started writing on a pad, and after twenty minutes into the story, Sam spoke up.

"Just a minute. I am going over to Dad's; I will be right back."

Sam left for his Mom and Dad's home nearby and came back in a few minutes. Sam handed Patricia and Wendy several newspapers.

Wendy and Patricia's eyes got big as saucers and their mouths fell open. "Special Edition: Dangers of Discipleship and Shepherding Movement Exposed."

Sam spoke. "This is what you are dealing with. This is from the perspective of Bible-believing Christians. This is a newspaper our families have published for years and continue to send all over the world warning churches about the discipleship teaching and how it can go wrong in a church. This is what I believe God wants you to know."

"Now I know why God wanted Mom to find you, Mindy. You have explained what is happening in our little church in Kittiburg.

"This is amazing. You have really helped us. Thank you so very much." Patricia was almost overwhelmed with thanks.

"Mom, what Pastor Jay is demanding of us in our little church is perverted discipleship designed to control everyone in the church body."

At a meeting with the district representatives, in the Kitty church, Pastor Slone swelled with importance as he gave his ultimatum. "The only issue that we will allow discussion on is whether the pastor and board have acted rightly in disciplining the two women."

"May I read this letter? Patsy asked.

"No! Sit down!" Slone ordered.

Justin stood and boldly spoke his request in defense of his two friends, Patricia and Wendy. "Can the two women be allowed to come to this meeting to face their accusers?"

"No! Sit down, Justin, you are out of order," Pastor Slone commanded.

"I think mercy and love need to be shown to these two women," pleaded Dean.

"Sit down! You are out of order!" Pastor Carpe, another district official, felt the need to add his voice of authority to keep control.

Eve, an eighty-year-old saintly woman, stood up and pleaded, "May I read what the Bible says about this?"

"No!" Pastor Slone quickly continued with his order, "Later! Like I said before, the only issue that will be allowed for discussion is whether the pastor and board have acted rightly in disciplining the women. The church bylaws are the ruling document."

About two weeks later, Wendy was sitting in her home looking out the window when a pickup turned into her circle driveway, stopped, and parked directly in front of her living room window. It was Pastor Jay sitting in the driver's seat of his car. He glared at her for about two minutes, spun his tires, and left in a hurry, throwing gravel onto the lawn. Wendy quickly closed her window blinds. She was frightened!

The following week, a group of cast out members and friends met again in Wendy's home for a time of fellowship, including singing and prayer. Pastor and Mrs. Couste, Pastor Prince and Princess, and a missionary couple from Honduras were present.

Justin felt the weight of responsibility as he declared what was on his heart. "We are all meeting here today to decide what action we should take and to have a time of fellowship. After attending and supporting my home church, as well as serving many years on the church board, I too have now received a certified letter from Pastor Jay stating that the pastor and board have reviewed my lifestyle and conduct and have decided that I am *out of harmony* with the leadership of the church. Consequently, Pastor Jay and the board have removed my name from the church roster. My wife can tell her own story."

"Yes," Patsy quickly agreed with her husband. "Justin and I both received excommunication letters. Because I have refused to attend the church since the public excommunication of my two friends Patricia and Wendy, I also have received a certified letter removing my name from the membership."

Pam, a policewoman, stated, "I am required to work some Sundays. Because my husband and I spoke up at the meeting in favor of letting Patricia and Wendy come before the church body, I also received a letter telling me that I am no longer on the church membership roster, and my husband was told his membership is in danger as well." Eve could no longer remain silent. "Like Justin, I am one of the founding members of fifty years, but that doesn't mean anything now. I have been told by Pastor Jay that I am not in harmony with him and therefore will not be allowed to teach the adult Sunday school class, nor be allowed to greet people at the door, nor be allowed to engage in any other ministry."

Bea joined the conversation, expressing her great concern. "A lot of young people have stopped coming to church. When they are asked why, they refuse to talk at first. But little by little, stories are beginning to leak out about the guilt trips, intimidation, and confidences being used against them in front of the whole group, being told to swear to keep secret the things 'God reveals' to them in meetings, and fear of what the pastor's wife will do if they ever tell anyone what is going on."

"Pastor Jay is telling people that they will die if they do not align themselves with him and his authority. They are afraid of confronting the pastor for fear of what he will do to them in return," said Wendy.

A portrait of where American Christianity has declined is displayed in the skullduggery of some clergy who have become inveterate hypocrites. Bullies in the pulpit are trying to take over the churches of today. If possible, these bullies who are controlled by their thirst for power and greed will rule and reign with cruel threats. They intimidate, manipulate, and coerce their followers (bully buddies) to gain absolute control.

> If my people, which are called by my name, shall humble themselves, and pray, and seek my face, and turn from their wicked ways; then will I hear from heaven, and will forgive their sin, and will heal their land. (2 Chronicles 7:14)

CHAPTER 4

The worship team had just finished the usual Sunday morning song service. Pastor Jay had finished making the announcements. After several months of dealing with pastoral abuse and the frustration of unanswered calls to the pastor, tempers were ready to explode. A church fight/scuffle broke out in the sanctuary between the pastor and the people who were demanding that Pastor Jay explain his false accusations, wild statements, and abusive actions. People stood up, and everyone tried to talk at the same time. Casidy and Shirley were quick to stand up and speak in defense of their friends.

"I would like to read two letters that you sent to my parents last week," pleaded Casidy.

"You are out of order, brother; sit down," Pastor Jay shouted in an attempt to show his authority.

"No. These letters need to be read to the entire church," Casidy responded.

Casidy started to move to the front of the church. When Pastor Jay saw Casidy moving forward, he shouted three more commands as he quickly started to move off the platform down to the altar.

Pastor Jay tried to cover his fear while speaking with as much authority as he could muster for the occasion, "This meeting is adjourned. Everyone go home."

Shirlene moved to the front of the church pleading with the audience, "People, you need to hear what he said about my mom and dad."

Pastor Jay moved off the platform and yelled, "Everyone pray! Pam, play the piano!"

Pam started pounding on the piano. Pastor Jay walked down the steps and knelt in front of the platform at the altar. He covered his head with his hands. About six to ten people walked to the front of the auditorium and stood in a half circle around the back of the pastor. They held out their arms and hands toward their pastor as a covering for his head, but they did not touch him. They started praying for him.

Casidy hurried onto the platform and headed for the mike to read the letters. Lynn, Jacob, and Johnny started shoving. Casidy was shoved several feet, almost off the platform. Shirlene hurried to turn off the mike at the piano and then turned on the mike at the podium so Casidy could read the letters.

Pam played the piano as loudly as possible to drown out the voices and all the confusion of everybody in the auditorium crying and talking at once.

Wendy quickly stepped onto the platform, sat down by Pam, and pleaded with her, "Please don't play the piano, Pam. This is very important; everyone needs to hear these letters. Please stop and listen!"

Wendy asked Pam, "Will you please stop playing the piano?"

In response to Wendy's request, Pam played the piano all the louder. Wendy gently touched the top of Pam's hands. Pam stopped playing the piano and shouted, "She is hurting me; please help me!"

Wendy looked at Pam and wondered if she was crazy. She removed her hands from Pam. At about the same time, Sal stepped upon the platform to help Shirley turn on the mikes.

Wendy saw that Casidy was being attacked, and someone had his arm around Sal's neck in a choke hold. After someone broke the choke hold, Sal walked over and fell prostrate on the platform floor right in front of his kneeling pastor to try and talk to him. Pastor Jay refused to remove his hands from covering his face.

"Pastor, please look at me!" Sal begged. "I want to know why you did this. What is bad about Justin's lifestyle?" After trying to get the pastor to look up and talk to him, he put one finger under Pastor Jay's chin and lifted his head to get him to look at him.

Ann and Patsy ran to the back of the church. Wendy left the platform and quickly followed Ann and Patsy into the church office. Ann hurried to the front of the desk, picked up the phone, dialed 911, and said, "Hello, this is an emergency. We need the police to come to our church immediately before anybody gets hurt. A church fight has erupted."

The police soon answered, "We are on the way."

Ann had just completed her phone call to the police when the pastor came running into his office and reached over the desk for the phone. "I have already called the police," Ann declared. "You are a whited sepulcher—a den of vipers." Then she walked out from in front of the desk toward the door.

Wendy started to follow her out. As she passed the pastor, she said, "I see snakes crawling all over you."

By this time other people were trying to crowd into the pastor's small office while Ann and Wendy hurried outside to meet the police.

Ann, the first one out of the church, cried out to the police, "I am so glad you have come. It was awful!"

A policeman started writing. "Tell me what happened."

"Pastor Jay and his wife quickly disappeared right after they saw me leave. They must have known that I hurried out of the church auditorium to phone the police. They know I am an executive secretary to the Kitty County commissioners and work at the county courthouse. The pastor has falsely accused people, and when he is confronted, kicks people out of the church. What took place in church this morning was terrible."

As people began leaving the church, the police asked for statements concerning the fight. Pastor and Mrs. Jay had disappeared and did not speak to the police.

About two weeks later, twelve of the people who attended the disruptive church service were served court restraining orders as directed by Pastor Jay and his lawyer with the backing of the church district officials. Thus, twelve people gathered and discussed their pastor's restraining order and the church brawl.

Wendy expressed her deep feelings of horror and disgust. "Did you see all of those outrageous and slanderous lies contained in the document that our pastor has signed under oath and penalty of perjury?"

"Yes! He can't get by with this," Ann informed her friends. "I work at the courthouse and have observed how the law operates."

"Really! Well, I also have been taking note of some questionable things," added Patricia.

It was still difficult for Wendy to believe that a pastor would kick someone out of a church for nothing, and especially her mother. Yet, she knew it really happened, and to make matters worse, the police now were involved as well. Almost out of breath, Wendy asked, "Did you know that two city officers were alerted to the possibility that there might be another fight or disturbance in the church?"

Patsy felt sorry for her friends and her husband, Justin. It was so difficult to see her friends unjustly hurt. "Pastor Jay has contacted the church officials and is receiving counsel and advice from one of the district church attorneys. Money paid to the church district headquarters too often is used to pay attorneys to defend district officials and pastors who are doing evil. Additionally, too often church money is used to silence other pastors who stand for justice and righteousness."

"It is so terrible and sad that our church leaders will only listen to one side," said Patricia.

"I think you need to know some of the things that are taking place because they are against you," continued Patsy.

"All right, Patsy, what else have you heard?" said Wendy.

"I hate to tell you, but I must. Rose Ann told me that our pastor is telling the people that he was assaulted and threatened, and that you, Wendy, groped Pastor Jay in his office."

"Patsy, you know that is totally false," declared Wendy in disgust and self-defense.

"I know. That is a very sick man! He needs help. It is awful!"

I Must Tell Jesus

I must tell Jesus all of my trials;
I cannot bear these burdens alone.
In my distress He kindly will help me;
He ever loves and cares for His own.

I must tell Jesus all of my troubles;
He is a kind, compassionate friend.
If I but ask Him, He will deliver,
Make of my troubles quickly an end.

Tempted and tried, I need a great Savior,
One who can help my burdens to bear.
I must tell Jesus, I must tell Jesus;
He all my cares and sorrows will share.

—Elisha A. Hoffman

CHAPTER 5

The Kitty church troubles were brought into the public arena. The court trial of the twelve people served with restraining orders had begun. Princess' friend Patricia asked Princess if she would be a character witness for her at their trial in district court in Kitty. Princess said yes. She was happy to help her friend. The courtroom was full. In addition, the hallway leading to the courtroom was lined with people sitting on chairs, as well as people standing on both sides of the hallway because of too few chairs. Two police officers were standing on guard to make sure there would be no altercations. Out in the hallway, Dina, Pastor Jay's wife, was going around and coaching people what to say on the stand.

Jaft Goman tried to keep Patricia from going back into the courtroom after leaving to go to the ladies' room. Patricia called to a policeman nearby to help her get back into the courtroom. Jaft later waved a packet of Kool-Aid in Patricia's face. He also handed Wendy a package of Kool-Aid. Wendy hurried down the hall to Ann, "Oh, Ann, see what Jaft gave me! I think this is a threat."

Ann quickly grabbed the Kool-Aid package, "Here let me have that. I will take care of him." She rushed down the hallway to a sheriff.

"Jaft Goman gave this package of Kool-Aid to Wendy. He is reminding her of the mass murder of nine hundred people who were poisoned by their cult leader, Jim Jones, when he made them drink his poisoned Kool-Aid."

The sheriff reached his hand out for the Kool-Aid package. "Give me the package, I will take it to the judge." He entered the judge's chambers and related the Kool-Aid story to the judge.

Judge Helms said, "Throw him out of the courthouse and order him to stay out if he does not want to be arrested. I will keep this package of Kool-Aid as evidence."

Pastor Jay's wife, Dina, was sitting at the back of the courtroom when a police officer standing close by, who did not know Dina, said to her, "Anyone looking at that man, Pastor Jay, can tell he is just a snake oil salesman."

"That *man* is my husband!" answered Dina.

The policeman was very quick to apologize. "Oh, I am sorry!"

In the courtroom, Ann, one of the twelve defendants, was dressed in a beautiful white flowing dress. A few minutes before the judge entered the courtroom, Ann flitted around from defendant to defendant giving last minute advice and counsel. She also conferred with their attorney.

Prince and Princess wondered why Rocky had driven across the state to attend the Kitty County Court hearing when it concerned another pastor's trouble—the restraining order against the twelve people who were excommunicated from the Kitty Church by their own pastor, Jay. Rocky's pastorate was many miles away. When Rocky spied Prince and Princess in the courtroom, he walked over to Princess and Pastor Prince, sat down next to Princess, and started speaking to her. He proceeded to ask some probing questions about who attended their church. Moreover, he declared, "District Superintendent Hank Sole sent me to the hearing in his place since he could be subpoenaed to court."

"Really!" Princess said, remembering his visit to their home. She could not help but wonder why Rocky was *really* attending the trial.

Soon the judge entered the courtroom, and it was time to start the proceedings.

The plaintiff's attorney called, "Will Wendy please come to the witness chair?"

Wendy stood and slowly walked to the stand.

Attorney Abe asked, "Wendy, are you one of the twelve that Pastor Jay is seeking anti-harassment orders against?"

"Yes."

"Wendy, did you make phone calls to parishioners telling them that they better not drink the Kool-Aid?"

Wendy looked directly at the judge and very emphatically responded, "I sure did!"

The judge grinned, and Wendy continued. "Pastor Jay was trying to control everyone and threatening the people if they didn't do what he said to do."

"Thank you. Let's move on. Did you grope Pastor Jay in his church office?"

"No! That is disgusting! How could I grope him when I had my purse in one hand and my Bible in the other hand? He is sick!"

"Wendy, will you tell me why you are here in court, today?"

"Because Pastor Jay told people in the church that since my mom didn't submit and come before the men of the church board, God had shown him my mom was going to die. That her heart would just stop, and she would just drop dead! He told me, 'I'm sorry you choose to align yourself with an evil spirit,' meaning, my mother. So, I thought I would warn my friends, as I did not want them to witness another Jim Jones massacre where about nine hundred people died from the poisoned Kool-Aid that their Pastor Jim Jones had served them."

"What does Jim Jones have to do with your case?" asked the attorney.

"Cults like those led by Jim Jones and David Koresh get started by situations like what has happened to our church flock. And I thought the people needed to be warned about the danger our congregation is facing. Like Jim Jones's congregation, after much abuse, fraud, and threats, hundreds of Pastor Jim Jones's church followers—about nine hundred people—were forced to drink poisoned Kool-Aid that their own pastor, Jim Jones, had poisoned so the people quickly dropped over dead. Those who refused to drink the poisoned Kool-Aid were shot on the spot. A very few managed to escape."

"Thank you, Wendy. I have one more question for you. Do you know why your pastor would say these terrible things to you?"

"Our pastor wants total power and control over the people. This sounds like another Jim Jones cult. Our pastor has threatened my mother and me and others in the church; you do as I say or else! He has kicked a lot of people out of their own church because they refused to bow and be brought under his evil control. Since Pastor Jay told my mother that she was going to die, that her heart would just stop, and she would just drop dead, I thought I needed to warn my friends. I didn't want my mother and friends to be poisoned by drinking our pastor's Kool-Aid, just in case it was poisoned!"

"Thank you, Wendy. That is all for now. Next, I call Justin to the chair."

Justin sauntered to the witness stand and was sworn in.

The plaintiff attorney asked Justin, "Can you tell us why you are one of the twelve defendants?"

"I don't agree with heartlessly kicking a widow and her daughter out of the church. I disagreed with Pastor Jay and the severity of the board's action and pleaded with the pastor to counsel with the women, Patricia and Wendy. Pastor Jay told me that if I aligned myself with Patricia, I would be aligning myself with an evil spirit and would die. Pastor Jay told me that Patricia, who is seventy-two, and I might die because of our wrongdoing. It was the board's intent to meet alone with Patricia and Wendy, and according to Pastor Jay, he needed to cast evil spirits out of them the same as the board members attempted to do to me at a later board meeting. I then verbally resigned from the board."

"What did the board attempt to do to you at that meeting?" asked the plaintiff attorney.

Justin was quick and very decisive as he answered, "Pastor Jay accused me of threatening his life. They laid hands on me and started praying real loud while trying to cast the devil out of me. I started praying louder for them—trying to cast the demons out of them at the same time."

"How many board members were there, and how was everyone treated by Pastor Jay?"

"Jacob, Johnny, Ray, Pastor Jay, and me. Everyone was upset. Pastor told me, 'You have demons in you. Can we pray for you?' I answered, 'Yes, if that is what you want to do.' They were all sitting down in chairs. Then they all got up and gathered around me and laid hands on me. They started praying real loud—then louder. Pastor Jay bent down and put his mouth to my ear, and his ear was real close to my mouth. I did not feel any demon's going out of me, and I knew I didn't have any. So, I decided the demons must be in the pastor, so I started praying for the pastor that the demons would come out of him. When the pastor got louder, I would get louder yet. And the demons started flying around the room. Then Pastor Jay asked me to leave the room. I told him *no!* Pastor then told the other three board members to go to the other building. So, they all got up and left. As Johnny and I were going out the door, he stopped and said to me, 'Justin, they are not treating you right.' I then got into my truck and left."

"Justin, thank you. That is all for now," said the attorney.

"Next, I call county commissioner John to the stand. John is a character witness for Justin."

"John what do you know about Justin's character?"

John enthusiastically spoke for his friend. "Justin would have to be sent to school to learn to lie. I have known him for a long time. He just does not know how to lie."

"Thank you, John. That is all for now." The attorney moved on to another witness, "Next, I call Ann to the witness stand."

"Ann, are you employed by the Kittiburg County commissioners?"
"Yes."

"Can you give us a short version of what happened to bring you here today as one of the defendants?"

"Absolutely! Pastor Jay tried and convicted a widow and a fatherless woman on gossip. Our constitution states that even murderers are presumed innocent until proven guilty, and they have the right to 'be informed of the nature and cause of the accusation; to be confronted with the witnesses against him; to have compulsory process for obtaining witnesses in his favor.' They are not convicted on hearsay. And no one is called to a hearing in a court of law without knowing what they have been charged with."

"Why are you one of the defendants?"

"Because Patricia and Wendy are my friends, and I do not know of anything that they have done wrong—except refusing to go to a board meeting without cause. Pastor Jay ripped our body apart—this same body that the Bible states is one of another, and if one suffers, we all suffer—this same body that Pastor Jay preached on for weeks about the importance of each part. This same church body is now bleeding to death internally."

"Do you know why your pastor was behaving this way?"

"He wanted to have control over the whole congregation. How could anyone, particularly a church board, sit in judgment on anyone else without any sound evidence—only hearsay? You don't just hear one side before you pass judgment—and that's what Pastor Jay did. Actually, he and his board didn't even hear the accusations; they just judged. Patricia and Wendy don't have enough time in this world to live out the hurt Pastor Jay caused them. He maligned their character, convicted, and executed them, and then he said he wanted a hearing. Why bother? The damage has already been done. Sounds familiar, doesn't it? Seems like Jesus had one of those same hearings before those great men of God—the Pharisees."

"Thank you, Ann. Next, I call Patricia to the witness chair. Patricia, would you please tell the court why you are here today?"

"Without any provocation or wrongdoing on our part, Pastor Jay took very extreme spiteful action against me and my daughter, Wendy. That night in June, Pastor Jay called me on the phone at 6:00 p.m. and told me to come to a board meeting the next night. I refused because Pastor Jay refused to tell me why. Only after I pressed him for a reason did he tell me anything. Then in anger he told me what he thought was wrong with me. He accused me of having a lying spirit and said that I had slandered everyone in the church. This was such a false accusation!"

"What happened next?"

"Pastor Jay told me, 'If you do not submit and come before the board and let us deliver you of this evil spirit, it means you will never be allowed to step your foot inside the church again.'"

"I said, 'Pastor, you can't do this.' Again, he told me, 'Don't you let me ever see you step your foot inside the church again.' Pastor Jay told people in the church that since I didn't submit and come before his men of the board, God had shown him that I was going to die. He said, 'Your heart will just stop, and you will just drop dead!' He accused me and my daughter of horrible habitual sin using the scripture about the 'man sleeping with his father's wife!' How could he by inference and suggestive insinuation imply we were guilty of sin, let alone such gross, horrible, detestable sexual sin?"

"Patricia, what reason would he have to say those things?"

"In Pastor Jay's excommunication sermon, he said that when this necessary spiritual purging begins to happen, he will cast others out of the church. I think Pastor Jay used Wendy and me as his first public examples to put dreadful fear into the people's hearts, so they would never dare to question or disobey him!"

"Thank you, Patricia. Now, I call Pastor Jay to the chair. Why are you seeking restraining orders against these twelve people?"

"Patricia and Wendy are sowing discord in the church, and I have received word that one of their friends, Henry, has threatened to kill me."

"Thank you, Pastor Jay. Now will Henry please come to the chair. Have you ever threatened to kill Pastor Jay or anyone else?"

Henry slowly boomed out in his deep voice, "No! I am a hunter, and I do own several guns. But I have never threatened to kill anyone, and certainly not Pastor Jay, although, he is trying to destroy several lives with his evil actions."

"Thank you, Henry. Now I call Delt to the chair."

"Did you threaten to kill Pastor Jay?"

"Of course not!"

"Thank you. Next, I call Patsy to the chair. Patsy, can you tell me why you are here in court?"

"My friends, Patricia and Wendy, have been falsely accused.

Pastor Jay has told people that they will die if they align themselves with Patricia and Wendy or anyone else who is being *disciplined* by him or do not go along with whatever he, the pastor, says."

"Thank you, Patsy. Now I would like to call Bea to the chair. Can you tell me why you are here in court today?"

"Confidences told to the pastor and his wife were used against the very people who told them as a means of guilt and intimidation. The pastor wanted total submission to his authority. Anyone who did not submit to him was in disharmony and risked being removed from the membership. I too came to Patricia and Wendy's defense."

"Thank you, Bea. Now I want to call Jimmy to the chair."

"Jimmy, did you assault Pastor Jay?"

"No! All I did was put my finger under the pastor's chin and lift his head up so I could look into his face when talking to him."

"Jimmy, did you have Pastor Jay's permission or approval to lift his head up with your finger?"

"No."

"Thank you, Jimmy. Now I call my final witness, Shirley, to the chair. Shirley did you stand up and help disrupt the church service?"

"I wanted to help my brother turn off the mike that was on the piano and turn on the mike that was on the podium so my brother could publicly read the two letters that Pastor Jay sent Justin and Patsy, my mom and dad."

"Thank you. This concludes my questions for now."

After a three-day, Thursday, Friday, and Saturday, hearing before him concerning the anti-harassment charges that Pastor Jay had brought against the twelve former members and nonmembers of the Kittiburg church, the judge rendered his conclusions.

"In conclusion, Pastor Jay did not prove his case, as only one of the twelve is charged with a one-year restraining order, because he, Jimmy, placed his finger under the pastor's chin and lifted his head up without the pastor's permission or approval.

"Based on the testimony heard, the exhibits admitted into evidence, and the arguments of counsel, the court makes the following findings of fact:

"That the petitioner has failed to establish that the eleven of the twelve respondents constitute a group who 'have planned together to use violence to disrupt church services' as alleged in paragraph 1.2 of the various petitions.

1. That the petitioner, Pastor Jay, has failed to establish that any of the above-named respondents threatened to kill the petitioner, as alleged in paragraph 1.2 and 1.3 of the various petitions.
2. That the petitioner has failed to establish that the above-named respondents "stormed the stage" of the church, as alleged in paragraph 1.3 of the various petitions.
3. That the petitioner has failed to establish that any of the above-named respondents "trapped" petitioner in the church office as alleged in paragraph 1.3 of the various petitions.
4. That no other act by any of the above-named respondents alleged in the various petitions constitute unlawful harassment as defined in RCW 10.14.020.

"Based on the above findings of fact, the court makes the following conclusions of law: That the petitioner has failed to establish by a preponderance of the evidence that the above-named respondents have committed acts of unlawful harassment or that good cause exists for the issuance of protection orders. Based on the above findings of fact and conclusions of law, the court hereby dismisses the petitions filed against the above-named respondents."

The judge then pointed his finger at Pastor Jay.

"Mr. Jay, you are a fabricator and a liar! And the people have a right to go back to their church in three weeks, if they so choose, after we get everything written up. Court is adjourned!"

The judge hit the gavel on his desk and left the courtroom.

This world is on the edge of moral decay. America's strength cannot rise above the righteousness and strength of her churches. Faithless and false leadership in the church leads to spiritual devastation and ruin not only for the leaders but for the people they lead. Many times people are balanced precariously between heaven and hell; thus, the truth must not be altered, watered down, or compromised, whether it be in the church or in the US government.

The church is not a place to hide your immoral and ungodly acts; thus, demonstrating false Christianity/spiritual hypocrisy. Instead, the church should stand for teaching, rebuking, and correction, all manifested through the love of Jesus Christ. This world is our testing, proving, and training ground for Eternity. The book of Revelation in the Bible teaches us that God requires true repentance and genuine restitution. "Remember therefore from whence thou art fallen, and repent, and do the first works; or else I will come unto thee quickly, and will remove thy candlestick out of his place, except thou repent" (Revelation 2:5).

CHAPTER 6

After the trial was over, the twelve respondents wanted to celebrate their victory at the Highway Lace Café for dinner.

Patricia wanted to show her appreciation for Princess' willingness to be a character witness in court. Thus, she approached Pastor Prince and Princess, "Thank you so much for taking the time to support me and my daughter in court. We would be pleased to have you as our guests at the restaurant. Will you two join us for dinner?"

"Honey, can we do that?" asked Princess.

Prince nodded his approval. "My wife and I will see you at the restaurant in a few minutes. Yes, we will join you."

"Princess, I really appreciate your willingness to be a character witness for me. And Pastor Prince, thank you for taking the time out of your busy schedule to attend court with your wife on behalf of all twelve of us who have been cast out of the church."

"You are most welcome. That is what we are here for—to help those in need."

"Patricia, I agree with my husband, we are happy to help you in any way we can. I am so thrilled and thankful for the outcome of that awful trial." Princess reached out to her friend with a loving hug.

"Yes, I am too. Thanks again. See you both at the restaurant."

In the car, driving to the restaurant, Prince expressed his concern to Princess, "We are happy to join them for lunch to celebrate their victory. But we both know that we will be rejoicing with the wrong crowd, the group that is under discipline by the district church officials, and as such, we run a risk of severe censure. Even so, I believe we are doing the right thing by saying yes."

"I feel the same way. I believe Jesus would help those in need. After all, they are our friends. Here's the restaurant."

In a few minutes, Patricia and her friends were seated in a private room in the restaurant eating and rejoicing over their court victory. Princess was sitting next to Patricia, and Princess' husband, Prince, was sitting on her other side.

Tears gathered in Patricia's eyes as she expressed her warm thanks to her dear friends, "All of us, the twelve cast out ones, thank you, our loyal supporters, for coming to the court trial and giving us your love and support. I want to especially thank Pastor Prince and Princess for consenting to be character witnesses for me. And thank you, Pastor and Princess, for coming to our celebration dinner."

Wendy followed her mother's lead with her own words. "At the deposition, the pastor lied under oath. And again these last three days in court, Pastor Jay continued to lie. But in the end, we won our case. Today, the judge dismissed all but one of twelve restraining orders. That one was issued because Jimmy did lay a finger on the pastor before the scuffle broke out. The judge, in his closing statements, told Pastor Jay that several of his statements in the petitions had been fabrications."

"Today is our day of victory. We have much to rejoice over," said Justin.

"Yes, thank you all for helping. I am so thankful to God and all my dear friends for their love and support," responded Patricia.

Prince and Princess were sitting around the table eating and rejoicing with their friends when suddenly, Judas Raide, one of Pastor Prince's deacons and a close friend of Rocky's, stood in the doorway taking mental note of all those present, including Pastor Prince and his wife.

"Oh, no!" Princess softly gasped and whispered to Prince, "Now we are in serious trouble with the district church officials! I am sure Judas is here in Rocky's behalf to take note and spy out the land."

"Honey, we are in the enemy's camp, which is a no, no!" Prince whispered to Princess as he continued to express his concern. "I still do not understand why Sole would send Rocky in his place. Since when did district church officials start helping a pastor kick people out of their home church?"

"Judas is one of your board members and is an old-time friend of Pastor Rocky. We both know that sometimes Judas even attends Rocky's church services in Everest," added Princess.

"I know! And I am sure Rocky has put a lot of pressure on Judas to force me to resign as pastor. Honey, we know too much about the corruption in which Rocky and some of the other district officials are involved."

Months later, Prince and Princess were discussing the events that followed the court trial of their friends. "Honey, it looks like we have been tried by a kangaroo court and found guilty. Remember, at the close of that terrible executive presbyters' meeting, while standing at the door, I asked Rocky, 'Have you talked to Judas about forcing Pastor Prince to resign his pastorate in Elliburg?'"

Rocky answered, "Yes, I told him to go to Dan Stone."

"And, of course, we know that Dan Stone is the one to oversee the Elliburg and Kittiburg churches, since he is the presbyter for the Kima section, which includes our church and your pastorate," said Princess.

"When Dan Stone was talking to us right here in our home, he said to us, 'There are no charges against either one of you.' Yet at the same time, he turns around and tells two of my board members and one other member to circulate a petition against me as their pastor. I don't understand what is going on! They must be really desperate to resort to such drastic evil maneuverings."

Princess was deeply concerned for her dear husband. "Honey, surely, Dan Stone knew that circulating a petition against a pastor would stir up discord, unrest, and bring confusion to the church that you pastor."

Prince, greatly perplexed, was searching for a logical answer as he responded to his wife, "I wonder what could possibly have made

Dan Stone act in such an un-Christian manner toward one minister/ pastor who had no charges against him, and on the other hand stand behind Jay, the neighboring pastor, who has many charges against him? It just doesn't make any sense."

"Honey, I think he is afraid to take a stand for what is right and honest. I believe he is trying to save his own skin because he is so deeply involved. In our earlier conversation, Dan told us that his church has given the Caring Outreach several thousand dollars, and 'this could be a big stink.'"

"I know. When the revealing light started to expose the corruption, it must have been rather frightening to the district officials to think of all the possible ramifications of the illegal activities connected with the Outreach ranch, including Rocky and various other district officials," declared Prince.

"Oh, honey, it is awful!"

"Ray Beade is the Caring ranch director; as well as a board member at the Kittiburg church, and his wife, Visha, is the church secretary/treasurer. One can readily see that this creates a very touchy situation. Possibly Rocky, Dan Stone, Del Carpe, and other district officials know that Pastor Jay or Ray Beade, either one or both, can expose some of the illegal activities that have continued to go on for years at the Caring ranch!" continued Prince. "Even so, neither sin nor the cover-up of sin ever pays!"

"It sounds like a most powerful, exclusive, and dominating group of men have taken over—these same church officials who are involved in this church corruption are an elite Mafia ruling within the church—bullies and bully buddies—a law unto themselves," Princess added emphatically.

"Undisciplined power corrupts completely! Yes, my honey, we need to cling to the Lord more than ever and trust Him to take care of us."

A few days later, Pastor Dan Slone, a district church official, phoned and asked Prince if he could come to see him. "I would like to talk to you. Would it be all right if I come to your home for a visit?"

Prince was quick to give a warm invitation. "Oh, yes, please do!"

"I will see you shortly."

A few hours later Slone rang the doorbell and was welcomed into their home by Prince. "Hello, Pastor Slone, come right in. Please be seated."

"Thank you, Prince. I asked to come here today to talk to you and your wife about you and your church and the district. How are you doing?"

"Not so good. I have a few questions that maybe you can answer. While attending the district council in Everest, it was revealed that the district was in the red about $3.8 million. The reason stated was, 'wrong accounting procedures with no fraud evident.' Is my understanding of this correct?"

Pastor Slone drew in his breath, "I know some things were wrong with the accounting."

"Nonetheless," Pastor Prince continued, "Rocky and the Outreach ranch at Kittiburg, received $515,000 in loans from the district revolving church loan fund for the falsely promoted illegal/fraudulent home mission's project, and, in addition, funded the $155,000 embezzlement. Why did the District Council officials, with Rocky leading the way, loan over half a million dollars to the illegal/phony Caring ranch deceptive ministry/cattle scheme when the district was in serious financial trouble?"

"I am not sure."

"We heard that Superintendent Hank Sole could have been fined $10,000. Is that right?" Princess significantly questioned Slone.

"We all could have; we still can be!" admitted Pastor Slone.

"Are there any charges against me?"

"No, Pastor Prince, there are no charges against you!"

"Are there any charges against me?"

"No, Princess, there are no charges against either one of you!"

"Then why all the threats against Prince, and why are you forcing Prince to resign as pastor, if there are no charges against either one of us?"

"I took Hank Sole's letter to Rob Gross, with a copy mailed to me, as a threat and a subtle hint."

"Well, I think you need to know that it was not so subtle."

Pastor Prince continued, "Two of my board members, Lee Fent and Melt Blake said, in a board meeting, 'Dan Slone told us to circulate a petition asking for Pastor Prince's resignation!' How could you do such a cruel thing to one of your own? How could you do this to my husband? Is this what you do to ministers who expose evil in the church leadership? We have come to the conclusion that all of you district officials are guilty of fraud and embezzlement because the district presbytery/officiary are Outreach board members, and you are defending the fraud and embezzlement that has been committed. Worse yet, you are cruelly and unjustly attacking the whistle blowers."

"I think you both understand that the district officials are serious, and it would be better for you if you drop this whole thing. We have now been talking for about one and a half hours; it is time for me to leave."

The Gate at the End of Things

Don't try to kid yourself with the thought
You can do as you please all the while;
Don't think you can kick the poor fellow who's down,
While you climb to the top of the pile.

Don't think you can fool all the folks all the while;
You may do it sometimes, that is true;
They will find you out in the end every time.
The only one you fool is you.

And you will learn what sorrow it brings
At the gate that stands at the end of things.

—Unknown

CHAPTER 7

Prince had a good board meeting until the verbal bomb was dropped by Melt Blake.

"Lane, Melt, and I had a meeting this past week with our district presbyter, Pastor Slone." With inflated importance, Judas Raide continued, "Pastor, we are sorry to have to tell you that Presbyter Dan Slone told us to circulate a petition asking for your resignation!"

Another board member, Lane Fent, added his fuel to the fire. "Otherwise, the district officials are going to come over and put you out. The district officials have the power and authority to do that. You have displeased them."

Pastor Prince turned white and humbly asked, "Isn't it enough that my wife and I are feeling the stress of the extreme pressure laid on us by the district officials without you, my own church board members, joining them in pressuring me to resign. You know that we recently had a wonderful church business meeting without any problems, and the people verbally expressed their love and appreciation for me and Princess, your pastor and wife. I do not understand why you are giving in to the district's unjust demands"

"This is orders from headquarters," Fent muttered. "He told us to ask our pastor to resign."

Pastor Prince's face was still white from the shock of hearing Judas's cruel announcement. He and Princess had been praying and believing God for a miracle. "I will do some praying and get back to you."

Lawrence, another board member, who is Pastor Prince and

Princess' son-in-law, spoke up in defense of his pastor and father-in-law and later wrote to the board members the following: "I just pray that the board members that are taking action against a man of God, that has done no wrong, will search their own hearts, because you will be held accountable to God for how you have acted. I will have no part in this action in trying to destroy a shepherd of the flock."

"I must do some more praying about all of this. I know the district is exerting pressure on you, and you are exerting more pressure on me to resign as pastor of this church, the church that I have faithfully pastored for ten years. I do not feel I should resign at this time, and I encourage you men to pray with me," said Pastor Prince.

"It is nothing against you personally," added Blake.

"We have to listen to the district officials," said Judas Raide, swelling with importance. "We have to do what they say—if you don't resign, they said they will come over here and put you out of this church as pastor—they have the power to do that. The district presbyter, Dan Slone, had a meeting with three of us board members, Melt Blake, Lane Fent, and me, in Yakima, where he told us to circulate a petition among the church members asking for your resignation as our pastor. We are sorry we have to do this to you."

"Thank you! We will trust God to lead and guide us," Pastor Prince humbly responded.

Later that evening, after the board meeting, sitting around the table in the family kitchen, Lawrence proceeded to give his version of what happened at the board meeting. "Mom you should have seen Dad when they dropped their bomb. Dad turned really white when they told him the district was going to come over and get him out. It was awful! It was terrible! I am through with them."

Princess' eyes filled with tears and compassion as she spoke. "Lawrence, I am so sorry you had to witness that. It is obvious that district officials have influenced the other deacons and have pressured them to join in their evil deeds against their pastor—my husband and your father-in-law. We love you so much and feel terrible that you must witness such cruelty."

Princess turned to her husband as he opened the back door and walked into the kitchen. She threw her loving arms around him as she spoke with deep concern. "Honey, Lawrence has been telling me about what happened at your board meeting. I am so sorry. What should we do, now?"

"I told them that I would pray about it. What is the use of trying to carry on as pastor of this church when the district officials are out to get me because we have exposed their corrupt deeds?"

About one hour later, Prince and Princess were in their bedroom preparing for bed, when again Princess threw her arms around her dear husband and with tears in her eyes spoke from her heart. "Oh, honey, I am so sorry. This is terrible. It is absolutely devastating. How could Pastor Dan Slone do such a thing to you? How could Melt Blake, Lane Fent, Judas Raid, and Earl Fent go along with the district officials' evil plot against you, to remove you as pastor?"

Prince drew Princess close to his heart in a very tender warm embrace, as he spoke softly to her. "My dear wife, thank you for your faithful love and support. I am so sorry you have to go through this terrible thing."

The family could not sleep until after midnight, and then fitfully. Princess turned over, snuggled deep into her husband's loving arms and finally went to sleep.

Prince and Princess were under heavy pressure—especially Prince. Two days later, Melt Blake phoned Pastor Prince again demanding another board meeting. "When are you going to resign?"

"I will let you know," Pastor Prince stated.

Later, Pastor Prince phoned Melt back and gave him his answer. "As I have said before, I am not going to resign now, and will you please pray?"

Lane joined Melt in harassing Pastor Prince with another phone call. "You haven't told us when you are resigning."

Prince stood firm. "I know the district officials are pressing three of my board members, including you, to force their pastor's resignation, but I am not resigning now. I am still praying about it."

Prince and Princess mailed their charges and petition for investigation against the district to the national headquarters'

Credentials Committee and mailed a copy to the District Credentials Committee by registered mail.

Later in the evening, Earl Fent phoned Pastor Prince. "Pastor, I would like to talk to you alone."

Prince and Princess needed to go to the Marsh's home and on the way stopped at Earl and Rita's. Earl talked to Prince in his outside shop while Princess visited with Rita in their home.

"I am not asking for a response from you now, but I wonder if it would be good for the whole church and your family as well, if next Sunday morning you publicly tell the people you will retire from pastoral ministry next January, when you are sixty-five. I want you to know I did sign a petition to get you to resign," said Earl.

On the drive to the Marsh's home, Prince told Princess what Earl had to say. "Honey, I don't think Earl has any idea how this pressure to resign as pastor cuts me deep. I don't blame him entirely—I think he is responding to all the pressure from the district officials because we have exposed their fraudulent church cattle scheme, embezzlement, and the whole corrupt mess."

"Ministers/pastors are not required to retire from public pastoral ministry when they turn sixty-five. I am sure what he said to you is inspired from the district officials, namely, Rocky. It is such a very strange request, especially when Earl has been so vocal about what a wonderful preacher and pastor you are."

"At our last board meeting, only a few months ago, there was no hint from anyone that they were dissatisfied with me as their pastor, and there certainly was no hint in any way of a petition stating the people wanted a new pastor."

"This pressure for you to resign as pastor by both the district officials and now by a few of your devoted board members is very cruel, especially, when you have faithfully pastored this church for ten years. What they are doing to you, your family, and your church is awful beyond words."

In the morning, Prince and Princess fasted and prayed at the church. Prince sensed that his hearing was becoming impaired, probably because of all the stress he was under.

Princess walked into Prince's home office early the next day and spoke to Prince, who was on his knees praying. He looked up and spoke in a sad voice. "Honey, my hearing is gone."

Prince stood up and Princess reached out her arms; they hugged and cried and prayed together.

"Oh, honey, I am so sorry. I love you so very much." They continued to stand with their arms around each other as they prayed together—their tears of sorrow mingling. Then Princess phoned some ear clinics and doctors' offices for an appointment with no success. A few family members and friends were praying for Prince's healing. Finally, she found a doctor who could see Prince.

Princess sat in the doctor's office silently weeping while the doctor examined her husband. At this time, Prince's hearing was a little better. Praise the Lord!

Finally, the doctor gave his assessment of what was wrong with Prince's hearing. "You have no infection and no wax. The ear clinic and hearing aids are the next move unless it gets better. If it gets better, then you won't need to go to the clinic. Stress can do strange things. From what you have been telling me, you have been under more than enough stress to cause a temporary hearing loss. Go home and rest. I think you will regain your hearing in a day or two."

"Thank you, Doctor. We have been praying, and I think my hearing does seem to be better already."

"Good! Be sure and get lots of rest and do not let anything worry you."

"Thank you. I will try. I feel better already."

Later that evening, lying in bed talking, Prince told Princess his good news. "Sweetheart, praise the Lord, God has restored my hearing. It steadily has been improving ever since we left the doctor's office! I give God the glory and thanks."

Princess snuggled into Prince's loving arms. "Oh, honey, I am so thankful. Praise the Lord for restoring your hearing."

"Yes, thank the Lord. I am grateful!"

Princess continued, "I feel your heartache. It is so awful what they are doing to you. I love you so much! You are such a wonderful pastor, preacher, teacher, loyal and faithful husband, father, and grandfather."

"Thank you, sweetheart! I am so sorry that you have to suffer. I never dreamed district church officials would carry on with their corrupt deeds and crucify the innocent instead of the guilty, and in so doing hurt my precious wife and family."

"Somehow, all things will work together for good because we love the Lord."

"Yes! Thank you for reminding me of that promise from God. My words are so inadequate to describe my love and feelings for you, my precious darling wife. I thank God for giving me such a good, loyal, loving, and faithful wife, mother, grandmother, and pastor's wife, all these many years. I don't know how many times I have told you before, but I am going to tell you once again, you thrill me beyond words; I love you so very much." Prince tenderly held Princess in his arms as he gently kissed her until she fell asleep.

Superintendent Barren Welock phoned Prince and requested a meeting with him, "We, the district executive presbyters—Felmer Kisch, Wes Lelk, Rocky Roleson, and I—would like to meet with you on May 18."

"I can meet with you on that date, but I would like my wife, Princess, to be with me."

You could sense the voice of superior authority flow from Welock. "I do not know if that would be proper as *you* are the credential holder, but I will see."

"I will think about it!"

After Prince thought about it for a while, he phoned Superintendent Welock back, "Since my wife has had more people and more information come to her, I think she should be there with me."

"I will set the ground rules," Welock sternly answered.

"I am not trying to set the ground rules," humbly replied Prince.

"Oh, yes, you are!" argued Superintendent Welock.

Prince quickly answered, "I will give it some thought."

A few days later, Princess was looking through the mail and handed Prince a letter. "Oh, honey, I think this is your written response from the district officials, to your 'petition for an investigation.'"

"Yes, this is their response to our charges of illegal activity. I will read it to you," said Prince.

Dear Brother Prince and Sister Princess,

In light of certain difficulties occurring over a period of time, and certain complaints you've registered concerning the district's executive officers handling of problems, plus your endeavor to involve General Headquarters to attempt a solution, you are hereby requested by the District Presbytery to meet with the Executive Presbytery at their ... meeting at the district office in Carland at 2:00 p.m. for dialogue.

It is urgent that you honor this appointment. Should you choose not to honor our request, further steps will become necessary.

As brothers and sisters in Christ, we're confident such matters can be brought to a satisfactory solution. We look forward to your response.

Sincerely,
Felmer E. Kisch, Secretary-Treasurer

Appointment Confirmation –

Yes, we will plan to attend the interview with the Executive Presbytery ... at the Northwest District office in Carland.

No, we will not be present at the ... meeting.
Reason for not attending.

In response to Felmer Kisch's letter requesting the Prince and

Princess' attendance at the executive presbyters' meeting, Prince and Princess drove to Carland for their 2:00 p.m. appointment.

Prince and Princess were kept waiting in the reception room for one hour past the scheduled time. While sitting in the foyer, Sal Beacon approached them, "Greetings! I am sorry that I must run. I have another appointment and will not be able to stay for your meeting with us."

"That is OK. We do have a package here with your name on it. My wife and I would like to give it to you since you must leave before our meeting starts."

Princess handed a thick package to Sal, "Here it is. Sorry you can't stay."

Craig Boston came out of the presbyters' room around 3:00 p.m. and led the couple into the room to meet with the eight district officials. Barren Welock, Felmer Kisch, Wes Lelk, Rocky Roleson, Del Carpe, Dan Slone, Justy Jep, and Craig Boston were present.

From the first contact by phone from District Superintendent Barren Welock, Prince and Princess clearly understood that this meeting was to discuss Rocky Roleson and his dealings with Caring Outreach. Not so! Superintendent Welock let the couple know in no uncertain terms that they were called in to discuss Prince and his credentials and to be interrogated by a kangaroo court, the district church officials.

Princess sensed the cold and unfriendly atmosphere hanging thick in the air. "May we tape this meeting?" she asked.

Del Carpe was very quick to answer, "Oh, no, we trust everybody around here."

Superintendent Welock did not offer to open the meeting with prayer but looked directly at Pastor Prince and plunged right into his evil/ungodly interrogation. "We are here to talk about you and your relational problem with the church. Have you heard the name Fread Floyd?"

Prince finally realized his credentials were truly in question and evasively responded, "If I answer that, it will just lead to something else."

Barren Welock fired his second arrow straight at his victim. "Have you talked to Fread Floyd?"

Princess, sensed where the meeting was going, and without flinching an eye, immediately came to Prince's defense. "We don't have to answer that."

Superintendent Welock was furious to be denied by a little lady, and in great indignation quickly pointed his finger at Princess. "You be quiet, I'm not talking to you, I'm talking to him." Furious, he then quickly pointed his finger at Prince and demanded of him, "What do you have to say?"

"The same as my wife; she's right!" Prince responded with a ring of triumph in his voice.

"Well, it looks like we're through then," a much-subdued Welock answered. Somehow his cocky attitude had vanished in front of the room full of men.

"Yes, I guess we are!" Prince agreed.

Princess knew this was their time to act; leaning over toward Prince and reaching for the attaché case sitting on the floor, she said, "Honey, before we leave, maybe now is a good time to give their packets to them?"

Prince and Princess leaned over and picked up the packets out of the attaché case and began passing them out to everyone.

The men started to open them. Suddenly, Superintendent Welock collected his flustered thoughts and tried to take authority again by commanding the men sitting around the table, "Don't open those now!"

Princess ignored Welock's command to the men; and proceeded to pass out the packets. "Wes, Del, and this one is unnamed. I'm sorry we didn't know your name, Craig Boston. We have filed formal charges like Brother Weede told us to. And the charges sent to the National Credentials Committee are against not only Rocky Roleson, but also against Hank Sole, Barren Welock, Felmer Kisch, Dan Slone, and Del Carpe."

"Why us?" Welock asked, not knowing what to think.

Prince, feeling a surge of confidence answered, "Because you didn't respond to our complaints and check into it like you should have. Because of the way you have handled our charges of illegal and fraudulent activity against the district officials, including Rocky and the Caring Ranch officials."

"Also, because of the threats we have received. Mann Dey said we are not on trial. The district church officials are the ones accused of documented/factual fraud," added Princess.

Superintended Barren Welock had regained most of his cocky self-assured authority and asked, "What does he know? When did you talk to him?"

Prince quietly answered, "We went to see him recently in Sunnybrook. He read everything, all the charges of documented factual evidence of affinity group fraud, embezzlement, government food commodity fraud, insurance fraud, real estate fraud, mail fraud, and wire fraud. Yet, the guilty parties have not been brought to justice."

"Why did you refuse to come to the May 18 meeting?" Superintendent Welock asked.

"I told your secretary that we felt we should wait until we received a response from the National Council since you said you wanted to talk about Caring Outreach," Prince answered.

Justy, the only presbyter who was friendly to Prince and Princess, spoke up in their defense. "Brother Welock, maybe I can clear something up. Mrs. Princess phoned me, and I told her to bring everything about Caring Outreach. Maybe I misunderstood."

"That's right. I told Justy that no one was paying any attention to us, and he told me to bring everything. Besides, Mann Dey told us we were not on trial," said Princess.

Rocky finally decided it was safe for him to speak and held up a pamphlet titled *Beware the Wolves.* "I understand you had some input into this."

Princess could hardly believe what she was hearing—she knew Rocky was throwing out a smoke screen to get them off the subject of lies and corruption pointed mainly at him. Thus, she answered without hesitation, "We read it, but we didn't know anything about it until after it was finished."

Rocky wasn't content with one deceptive/false smoke screen but threw another one. "We might have to sell the ranch because of what you've done."

Prince, feeling a new surge of confidence from the Lord, declared plainly, "No! It is because you and the rest of the district officials are conducting an illegal, fraudulent operation. It is not a ministry but an illegal cattle scheme for which church contributions are solicited."

Presbyter/Pastor Dell Carpe decided it was time to join Rocky in throwing false/deceptive arrows at Pastor Prince. "People from your church are phoning us."

"About whom?" Prince asked.

"About you," smugly answered Dell.

"What can you expect, when district officials urge my deacons to circulate a petition against their own pastor and urge my board members to give me, their pastor, an ultimatum—resign or the district will come over and force me, as their pastor, out of the church?" declared Pastor Prince in self-defense.

Princess knew it was time to defend her husband. "A couple of our deacons said one of the district presbyters told them to circulate a petition asking for Prince's resignation, even though there were no charges against him. Some of our people said a board member tried to pressure them into signing a petition, but they refused."

"Compare the district's treatment of me, Pastor Prince, by district officials, with no charges against me, to the district supporting and backing my neighbor, Pastor Jay, in his evil/gross sins that were proven to be true in a court of law."

Superintendent Welock decided too much was being revealed and said, "We are going to close in prayer." He did not open the meeting in prayer, but it made it easier to stop the meeting by calling for a prayer. He then prayed a brief prayer in closing.

Prince and Princess stood up to leave; all the men joined them by standing up to say goodbye. Prince and Princess walked out of the room, left the district office, and headed toward the restaurant for their scheduled meeting with news reporter Fread Floyd.

CHAPTER 8

At another church board meeting, Melt Blake declared, "Pastor Prince, you have to resign next Sunday."

"If you don't resign next Sunday, you will have to announce that a special business meeting will be held on June 21," declared Leen Fent.

Melt tried to soften the blow, while at the same time shooting another arrow at his target. "We assure you, Pastor Prince, we have nothing against you, but a business meeting will be chaired by district officials June 21, for the sole purpose of voting you out as our pastor."

"I will pray about it some more, but most likely I will resign next Sunday or have someone else read my resignation," Prince responded in a very somber voice.

Later that evening, Princess tried to comfort her husband. "All this pressure to resign your pastorate—coming from the district officials and now from your church board members—is affecting your health and is downright cruel. The terrible threats from district officials and now from two of your main board members are cruel and unfair; besides, it is making us both sick at heart."

"I'm sorry, honey, but I do need to resign this next Sunday, or the district officials will literally take over with a rod of iron. And that will be harder on our church people as well as harder on our health and our family. I am so sorry you must suffer through this."

Tears were running down Princess' face as Prince gathered her into his loving arms. "Oh, honey, I am so sorry for you, too. And all our precious children have to suffer with us."

"Oh, honey, I am so sorry! But remember we still have the Lord and each other's love, and our precious children's love. And you are such a comfort to me; you thrill me beyond words. I am so grateful to the Lord for giving me such a wonderful wife and loving companion," said Prince as he tried to comfort Princess in a very loving close embrace.

"Thank you, honey. I don't know what I would do without your comforting love and prayers. We are blessed despite our present circumstances."

A few days later, Sunday morning, Prince and Princess were in their bedroom dressing for church.

"Honey, I believe this is the saddest Father's Day of our lives."

"I agree! It will be exceedingly difficult to preach a farewell message under these circumstances. I am so thankful our dear, loyal children have come home to help us."

"Yes! They are all so very precious to us. God has blessed us with wonderful children. They are so loving, sweet, and loyal to us and have come to honor, support, and help us in our very sad Father's Day farewell church service." Princess' eyes filled with grateful tears as she continued, "They are such good sports. I am so happy they were able to come. I know they will be a blessing and an inspiration to you as you preach."

"Yes! We have much to be thankful for. Praise the Lord for His gift of our children's and grandchildren's love and support. I am very grateful they are going to sing some of our favorite songs. Yes, it will really help me; also, I am so very thankful our daughter, Dawn, is willing to play the piano for this morning's farewell service as well as playing for the special songs our family will be singing. I know it will be hard on them to do so. Bless their dear hearts. We love them so very much.

Later in the morning service, Prince read his resignation to his very tearful church congregation, as well as to some dear friends and to their precious children, who had come to honor Pastor Prince and Princess, their dad and mom, in a sad and tragic Father's Day goodbye service.

"It is now ten years since we came to minister as pastors. During that time, we have sought to be faithful to God and to each one whom we have had the opportunity to minister to. In His faithfulness, God has blessed in saving souls, filling believers with the Holy Spirit, healing the sick, and lifting the fallen. Without *Him* we can do nothing.

"The time has now come to resign as your pastors. Separation from ministry responsibilities is never easy, given the best set of circumstances. Today is no exception. As always, there are mixed emotions on the part of many.

"The reasons for resigning at this time are varied. Due to extenuating circumstances—some beyond our control—we shall be closing out our ministry today at Elly Church.

"We express our gratitude publicly for the opportunity of ten years of ministry in this assembly. Our future and yours is in God's hands. It is to Him that each one of us shall give an account.

"We close with the words of the Apostle Paul to the Corinthian church: "The grace of our Lord Jesus Christ be with you all. My love be with you all in Christ Jesus. Amen."

"Because of Jesus!"

Pastor Prince and Princess

After the service, walking across the church parking lot to the parsonage, their home, one of Prince and Princess' dear little grandchildren, Joseph, looked up to his mother, Mary, and in a serious little voice said, "Why are they kicking Grandpa out?" Joseph's mother looked down to her young son, and with a sad, hurting heart answered her little boy, "Somebody real mean is doing this to Grandpa."

CHAPTER 9

Prince started having chest and arm pains on July 19, 1995, at six o'clock in the morning while watering the lawn of their daughter Eunice, for whom they were house-sitting. He did not say anything to Princess about it but continued watering the lawn and flowers.

Around 11:30 a.m. Prince walked into the house and in a very weary voice spoke to Princess. "I'm tired and want to go upstairs and lie down awhile."

"How about lunch?"

"Do I have to eat?"

"No! We can eat later. Honey, I hope you didn't work too hard out in the heat. It is an extremely hot day. You go get some rest."

"Oh no, I just need to lie down for a nap. You can call me when lunch is ready. Thank you for understanding."

Princess decided to wait with the preparations for lunch until her husband was through resting. She did not have long to wait, for Prince soon called from upstairs.

"Honey, come here!"

Princess knew something was wrong and called out as she hurried up the stairs, "What's wrong?"

A feeble voice answered, "I don't know!"

Princess' feet took flight, as she flew up the rest of the steps, not knowing what to expect. She definitely knew something was wrong. Her heart quickened when she found Prince lying on the bathroom floor.

"Honey, what's wrong?"

"I have pain in my chest and arm, and I almost passed out." Prince had not been able to sleep so arose to shave; and while he was shaving almost blacked out. Immediately he got down on the floor. He tried to get up and continue shaving but broke out in a cold sweat and ended up on the floor calling for Princess to help him.

Immediately Princess laid hands on Prince's head and started praying for him; simultaneously she reached for a damp washcloth to wipe off some of the shaving cream still on Prince's face. Her touch discovered he was cold and clammy, and his T-shirt was drenched with perspiration. Before she was through praying Princess asked, "Shall I phone 911?"

"I don't care!"

Princess knew his physical condition had to be serious for Prince to respond this way. This was the response Princess needed for her to take command of the situation. She felt weak and shaky but gathered strength from above for the strenuous hours ahead of her.

The 911 operator was kind, patient and gentle with her as he reassured her that the ambulance and paramedics would be there right away.

"I will stay with you on the line until they arrive. Do not let your husband go to sleep. Keep his head down," said the 911 operator.

Princess thought 911 operators only talked to little children this way and other people in very dire emergencies. She was so grateful and thankful to him for his kindness to her.

"I will ask my husband for the address."

The 911 operator quickly assured Princess that they already had the address. "That's all right, I have it right here on the computer. The men will be at the door any minute."

The paramedics and ambulance arrived in about five minutes. Four men worked to stabilize Prince. Immediately, they started administering IVs to Prince while taking his blood pressure, pulse, and whatever else was necessary. The head paramedic told Princess, "You can ride in the front of the ambulance."

They transported Prince as quickly as possible to the closest hospital.

Not long after, Prince was admitted to the hospital; since the pain would not cease but went from one arm to both arms besides his chest, it was diagnosed as a heart attack. The pain left shortly after the clot buster was administered to him. He was put in the intensive coronary care unit with a cot provided for his wife to help take care of him, according to his wishes and request.

The next day, soon after Prince was transported to the Intensive Coronary Care Unit, Princess looked up to see Rocky Roleson and Wester Lelk standing in the doorway of the Intensive Coronary room. Prince's enemies had come! Her heart quickened, and she wondered if Prince would be able to stand the added stress of their appearance at this time.

Rocky was the spokesman. "We met one of the requirements; there's two of us." The other requirement for the intensive care unit was only family members.

After a few minutes of conversation, Rocky reached to take hold of Prince's hand, and his other hand took Princess' hand, while Wester, on the other side of the bed, took Prince's other hand.

"Let's pray," said Wester. Then he proceeded to pray for Prince. Soon after, they said goodbye and left the room.

After Wester and Rocky left the hospital room, Prince and Princess discussed their visit.

"Honey, I was warned by the Lord that possibly someone from the district office would come in to see me," said Prince.

"I certainly had no warning. Maybe it was just as well. I am going to talk to the doctor about their visit. You cannot have visitors come in and distress you," replied Princess.

Later that day, Princess told their doctor about the stress their family had been under for almost three years and about their uninvited visitors. The doctor indicated that the nurse would immediately take care of things by limiting visitors to only Prince and Princess' children; all calls would be carefully screened.

Prince was moved from the Intensive Coronary Care Unit to the Progressive Coronary Care Unit; both units were called critical care units. Prince and Princess' children were permitted to visit with their father in the critical care unit.

Many tears were shed, and hugs were given as this was a shock to their dear family. The family's tearful and emotional yet very wonderful family reunion in the hospital included Willy, a close police friend of the family. They were so grateful that the doctors did not limit the number of children and grandchildren that could be with their dad and mom in the hospital room at one time.

Doctor House performed an angiogram on Prince at Hope Hospital on July 24, 1995. Later, he came to the room and gave his report to Prince and Princess. One place in Prince's heart artery was 80 percent closed. The doctor advised angioplasty (balloon) to take care of the problem. He informed the family of the various risks involved in this procedure. Prince took the doctor's advice and said he could do what he felt was best.

Princess told the doctor, "I believe you are God's gift to us. Thank you so very much!" Both Prince and Princess felt the ever-abiding presence of the Lord with them and knew God was the one who really was in control. Praise the wonderful name of Jesus. Thank the Lord for His marvelous miracle of love and grace!

Around 7:00 a.m. on July 25, Prince was moved by ambulance to Providence Hospital in Seattle. Again, according to Prince's desire and request, Princess rode along in the ambulance. The angioplasty did not work on Prince. When the balloon was removed, the artery collapsed to 90 percent closed. Thus, Doctor House, after consultation with other surgeons, implanted two stainless steel stents in Prince's heart artery.

Prince spent the next three days, July 25 through July 28, 1995, in the critical care unit at Providence Hospital with his wife close by his side, daily reading the Bible to him, praying for his recovery, and doing what she could to assist the doctor and nurses. Prince and Princess so keenly felt the sweet presence of the Lord with them all the time.

On the evening of the twenty-eighth, Prince was moved out of the Critical Care Unit to another recovery room, hopefully to be released the next morning. The next day, after Doctor House took Prince for a short walk around the hospital hall, he released him to go to the home of their daughter, Eunice, with instructions to come back to the doctor in two days, then again two days later, and once each week for the next few weeks, for a checkup. Eunice's home was close to the doctor's office, and the hospital was also close by, which was a real help in going to the doctor for the follow-up examinations.

Prince and Princess' youngest son, Jonathan, was able to make the trip over the mountains and spent the weekend, alone, with his father and mother at Eunice's home.

Bless the Lord, O my soul, and forget not all his benefits;

Who forgiveth all thine iniquities; who healeth all thy diseases;

Who redeemeth thy life from destruction; who crowneth thee with lovingkindness and tender mercies;

Who satisfieth thy mouth with good things; so that thy youth is renewed like the Eagle's. (Psalm 103:2–5)

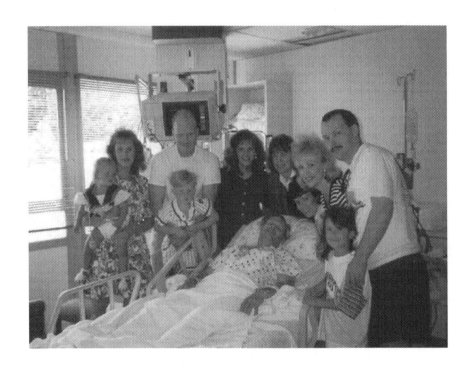

When Jesus comes for his bride:
All sorrow and crying will flee away.
This is the day the Lord hath made, we will rejoice
and be glad in it.
Whosoever will may come.
Praise the Lord!

CHAPTER 10

After over two months of healing, October 8, 1996, Prince and Princess visited with Pastor Richie in his church office at Colt, Washington, from 11:15 a.m. to about noon.

"News travels fast. Rocky phoned me from the district office and made it clear that I better not have you or your wife help in my church again," said a very concerned Richie.

"How did he know we helped you with your church service?" responded Prince.

"Someone told him that you, Prince, led the worship service and Princess played the piano in my church a few weeks ago. If anyone sees you here, today, right now, here in my office, I will be in big trouble!"

"That's what I was concerned about. Other ministers and different people who have anything to do with my wife and I, have been threatened as well. Some have really suffered as a result. Our friends, Ren and Benie, lost their positions in the church they had helped build. Their family has greatly suffered because they dared to question the district officials concerning the fraud and as to why I was excommunicated from the fellowship for exposing the district officials' guilt," responded Prince.

"It sounds like they are desperate," said Princess.

"I agree with my wife; I think they are. I am really sorry this has happened to you, Richie."

Princess remembered telling Richie to read their book. "That's why I told you, Richie, to read our book, *Whited Sepulchres.*

Primarily, because we wanted you to know what was going on before we ministered in your church. We are so sorry for you."

Richie appeared to be extremely nervous and kept looking out of the window. "I know!" he said. Thoughtfully, Richie continued. "I need to tell you something. Because I told Rocky that I did not know anything about your book, he then, said to me, 'Since you were ignorant, neither your credentials nor your church is in jeopardy.' I had to ask God to forgive me for lying to Rocky. Now, I know my credentials are in jeopardy!"

Prince couldn't help but feel sorry for Richie as he spoke with compassion and concern. "I am very sorry that this has happened to you."

"I believe the documentation presented in your book *Whited Sepulchres* is true. If it were false, there would be no need for the district officials to intimidate ministers or forbid them to read the book."

"It most definitely is the truth," Princess emphatically answered.

"I am very concerned about my position in the Colt Assembly due to my evaluation by the district officials as pastor of a Home Missions church. However, I believe that the people in my church will pull their church out of the council if the district officials try to remove me as their pastor and the district will be left with the building debt."

Prince remembered the cruel hand of the district officials as he spoke. "I trust it does not come to that."

Princess, also, could still feel the evil blows coming from the district church officials and spoke from experience. "Too often church leaders become a powerful, exclusive, dominating group, a law unto themselves."

Richie continued. "I asked Rocky if the Feds were doing an investigation on him and the other district/Caring officials. His answer was, 'Oh, no, Brother. That's a total fabrication.' According to what you are saying, Rocky did not tell me the truth."

Prince gasped. "No, Rocky was not honest with you. The fact is, the Feds most definitely are investigating Rocky, and the Caring Outreach, including other district officials, and others involved. If

Rocky made that statement to you, he was not speaking the truth; what he said was absolutely false."

"Two criminal IRS agents, an FBI agent, and two attorneys from the US Justice Department in Washington, DC, have all been in our home asking questions and taking copies of documents concerning the Caring Outreach fraud/embezzlement," said Princess.

"I am sorry that Rocky continues to deceitfully cover his guilt of fraud and embezzlement," added Prince.

Richie continued to be nervous and worried as he spoke. "I think I understand a tiny bit of how you feel, because I too, have now become the brunt of his cruel power."

"Our prosecuting attorney and our head sheriff have turned the Caring Church fraud case over to the FBI for investigation. The criminal IRS agents had already been investigating the outreach embezzlement and fraud case for some time before the FBI became involved," continued Princess.

"As a result of whistle blowing, we were forced to leave our ten-year pastorate, and then I was dismissed, excommunicated from the denomination, after forty-seven years ministering as a minister within the denomination. I think they became very angry with both of us for exposing the Caring fraud and embezzlement in our book *Whited Sepulchres,*" said Prince.

"That book reveals the truth about the mail fraud, wire fraud, and embezzlement that the district officials and Caring Ranch personnel et al. were involved in," added Princess.

As though the light bulb suddenly turned on, Richie said, "It is not hard to understand why they are angry; you have revealed their guilt to the public."

"Yes," answered Prince, "Isn't it a crime to misuse government funds, receiving US government food through deception, and then use the government food to feed the wealthy instead of hungry children or the poor who need food to survive?"

"It certainly is a mess, isn't it? I am sorry I lied and had to ask the Lord to forgive me when I denied any knowledge concerning you and your book. However, I do believe what you are telling me is true."

"Yes, it is true. We have firsthand experience and knowledge," explained Prince.

"But," continued Richie, "I have a concern about how long before the issues you relate in your book will be resolved. Three of my church families have indicated they want nothing more to do with our church denomination because of the district officials' fraudulent deeds. I am going to attempt to calm them."

"I know; it seems like forever! We are now attending the same church that we were forced to leave after Prince's ten-year pastorate. At times, it has been difficult, but we love the pastor and his wife, and still love the same people who were used by the district officials to help force us to leave. I have discovered through experience that God's times are not always our times. God is in control, and I do know that He will eventually bring justice in His time!"

Princess gave her husband a knowing look, "Yes, honey, I agree with you, although sometimes it is hard to wait for God's time. Our daughter, Lynn wrote in the foreword of *Grand Jury Mystery*: 'Today, too many pastors are so caught up in their leadership and their congregations lining up with their authority, which they believe is a direct line from God, that living with integrity or being beyond reproach is left behind.'"

"Yes," pondered Richie. "I am ashamed of my conduct. Where is the standing up for what is right? You are so fortunate to have grown children who understand, love, and support you in what you do, even though sometimes it is not popular with the crowds."

"Richie, we understand your fear of becoming involved. We know of others who have also suffered at the hands of ungodly church leaders. My wife and I have personally become acquainted with Derek, a young intern in a large church. Apparently, he was soon to be on staff as the youth pastor, which promotion was suddenly stopped because he reported a crime of embezzlement (hundreds of thousands of dollars) by the head pastor. After he exposed what he had witnessed to the District Officiary, he then became the target of their church leaders' evil abuse. As a result of exposing the embezzlement, Derek was beaten up in the very same church building that had been his spiritual sanctuary, then he was expelled from his church, left homeless, and on the run for his very life."

"That is so awful! Yet, at the same time, I am so glad that you understand me in my weakness and eventual sin. Now I ask you to forgive me for lying and not taking a stand for righteousness and on your behalf," pleaded Richie.

"Of course we forgive you," Prince quickly responded.

"Yes, we do forgive you and, also, we reach out our arms of love and forgiveness to all of our other minister friends who have not had the courage, like you, to ask us for forgiveness," added Princess.

"I am certain it has been and still is very painful to be excommunicated and deserted by your church family of many years. I am so deeply sorry you have had to suffer this awful, unjust tragedy," said Richie.

"I appreciate your thoughtful words. Thank you! I admit it has been and still is a very painful thing to have experienced. But God has been so wonderful and faithful to both my wife and me and our precious family who have also suffered with us. I know He will continue to uphold and sustain us through all the trials and tests of life that we are asked by God to endure."

Some days later, Prince and Princess were in their home eating lunch when the mail arrived. Princess stopped and handed a letter to Prince. "I thought we were prepared for this. But I guess we are not, because I have a terrible sick feeling."

After reading the secretary's letter from national headquarters, Prince sat stunned. His emotions were running wild; he felt the wounds cut deep. He slowly handed the letter back to Princess to read herself. "Well, they have dismissed me from the fellowship; they have removed me from their ministerial roster. My name is on the 'scandal sheet'—the 'blacklist.' However, I am thankful I was already accepted as a minister with another denomination before I received this dismissal letter. It helps to ease the sting a little bit."

"I am so sorry this has happened to you. Yes, I am thankful, too, that we are part of another ministerial organization. But it still hurts!

I never dreamed they would excommunicate you from the fellowship that we have been a part of for so very many years. And they knew full well what you stood for and continue to stand for, as well as what I stand for. Yet, they proceeded with their cruel plans, all because we exposed their evil deeds."

"I know, honey! And, yes, it does sting to know I have been betrayed and deserted by those so close, men who are of the same household of faith. Thank the Lord that they do not have any power to remove me or you from God's heavenly roster."

Princess continued talking out of the depths of her broken heart. "Yes, that is so true. What a comfort! I am thankful too. Now it is starting to make sense, what Superintendent Welock told me over the phone only a few days ago, 'We have tried several times before to do this to Prince, but you always circumvented us.' Remember when you were still in the Critical Coronary Unit you received that awful letter from Superintendent Welock demanding your presence at another district presbyters' meeting. Welock had to know that letter would be stressful to you."

"It is tragic that some of our church officials have committed illegal acts, but more tragic is the covering up. I do not understand what is wrong with some of our church leaders," said Prince.

"I wonder if Superintendent Welock was trying to intimidate you or cause you to have another heart attack and die in the hospital. I never dreamed they would treat you this way for exposing their own illegal deeds, their own corruption, but they did," continued Princess.

Prince tried to reassure Princess, "Remember, dear, God is still in control; all the other times they were unable to succeed in their evil plot against us because God would not let them. I was grateful for my doctor's letter to the district superintendent. In his letter to them, he informed Superintendent Barren, 'I cannot allow Prince to resume any business or church-related activities at the present time and have advised him not to attend the upcoming meeting on February 13, 1996.' Honey, remember, you told Superintendent Welock that my doctor would not release me to attend any more of their district presbyters' meetings until he knew I had sufficiently recovered from my severe heart attack."

"That is right! Yet, despite the doctor's orders, they went ahead and dismissed you anyway and worse yet, when you could not appear to defend yourself. How evil can they be? We have been threatened so many times to *'be quiet or else!'* I wonder if maybe in their desperation the district officials really did want to do you in by causing you to have another heart attack. At least that is what appears to me; they have desperately tried to do just that—destroy you and me in one way or another to save themselves. After hundreds and hundreds of ministers read our book *Whited Sepulchres*, the ministers soon started demanding answers from the church officials. Rather than give them honest answers, they have lowered themselves to dishonest answers and to *save face* have desperately tried to do away with both of us."

"God will not let them. We belong to God, and not to them. Praise the Lord!" declared Prince.

**The
Elite Mafia Rules:
Muzzle the Messengers
at Any Cost**

***

The most powerful, exclusive, dominating
group—a law unto themselves

***

**But the Messengers
Refused to Be Silenced**

***

CHAPTER 11

"Whosoever will may come." Faithful is the Lord, who has promised, "Lo, I am with you always," and "I will never leave thee nor forsake thee."

Prince and Princess, still floundering and reeling from what had transpired, continued to float around looking for a church home. Upon finding a church in which they felt comfortable, they attended it on a regular basis for about five years. They sometimes helped serve Communion, receive the offering, and read the scriptures. Prince, also, taught the seniors' Sunday school class.

Prince and Princess received letters and verbal messages from the senior pastor urging them to join the church. Prince was asked to consider the position of a church elder. Then one day, rather suddenly, Rad, the youth pastor, was dismissed and fired. Senior Pastor Tilt informed Rad that he was no longer welcome in the church, and the police would arrest him if he set foot on the church property. Pastor Tilt helped destroy Rad's marriage as well. Rad was really suffering—he was in severe pain and on the verge of utter despair.

In his great distress, Rad came to Prince and Princess' home for help; their home became a place of refuge in his time of need. Prince and Princess felt his pain, suffered with him, opened their arms of love and prayer, and gave him a haven to which he could flee anytime for shelter, day or night. Rad slept on their couch, slept in one of their beds, ate at their table, and received their open arms of unconditional love, comfort, and prayers. Rad was in desperate need of help and comfort. Prince and Princess were only doing what they had been doing for years and years—ministering to the needy and binding up their wounds.

Then one day, Prince and Princess received a phone call from Pastor Tilt, who informed them, "I hear you are lodging with Rad, and if you are lodging with Rad, you are no longer welcome in *my* church." Several threatening phone calls from Pastor Tilt to Prince and Princess followed.

Soon thereafter, a policeman stood at their door and told Princess, "Pastor Tilt sent me here to tell you that you are no longer welcome at *his* church, and if you go to *his* church, you will be trespassing."

Prince and Princess were threatened with a charge of trespassing if they attended the church they had been attending for years, where they worshiped God with their family and friends, all because they were doing what they had been called to do—minister to the wounded. Yes, Rad was lodging with them because he was deeply hurt and in great need. Yes, they were feeding Rad as well. Prince and Princess were doing what they believed Jesus wanted them to do—show love: "Bind up the wounded and bleeding and feed them."

Various times before, Pastor Tilt had used the police to do his bidding—to harass, threaten, or intimidate various other individuals in attempting to take care of his internal church problems, thus controlling the people who attended his church.

The next Sunday, after Pastor Tilt's evil order had been delivered to the family by way of the city police, church elders stood on guard at all the church door entrances. Their son, Jonathan, agreed to be a friendly church spy for us, and he witnessed the men with hand phones—walkie talkies—stationed at all the doors inside and outside of the church building. This was an exceptionally large church congregation, close to one thousand, more or less—three Sunday morning services to accommodate all the people.

Yes, Prince and Princess did write letters to the city prosecuting attorney, county prosecuting attorney, city attorney, chief of police, mayor, city manager, city council members, county commissioners, head sheriff, Washington State attorney general, managing editor of the *Daily Record*, as well as several hundred church members, but no one responded to the letters. Those who understood knew that anyone who dared get on the wrong side of Tilt or who had the audacity or gall to stand up to him could expect to be the brunt of his ruthless wrath. Prince and Princess got on his blacklist in November 2000, around Thanksgiving time, when Pastor Tilt found out that Prince and Princess had befriended one of his victims.

Prince and Princess realized they could have used their son-in-law, Joe, who was a state patrolman for twenty-six years, to harass Pastor Tilt, his elders, or any other people with the threat of a speeding citation, or a no trespass warning, or maybe even an arrest if they displeased Prince or Princess. But they refused to do so because they knew it would not be ethical. Just because the couple's son-in-law, Joe, worked with the US marshals, Prince and Princess knew that would not give them a right to use the US marshals to harass Pastor Tilt or any of the elders on the church board. Their answer was no, never!

Prince and Princess could have sued Pastor Tilt and the police, big-time, but they chose not to do so. They documented it in a book, instead, and left it in God's hands! Besides, they were so wounded themselves that Prince ended up in bed again—first from the Assembly wounds and then from a different church denomination. Fresh new wounds were inflicted by Pastor Tilt, his ungodly elders, and his police henchmen. Freedom of religion, freedom of worship, freedom of speech, freedom of the press, and separation of church and state were all violated.

Prince and Princess' Christmas plans and Christmas peace were disrupted because the police took orders from a private citizen, Pastor Tilt, who sent the police to the family's house without any legal right—no letter, no trespass warning, and no cause of any kind—just, "Pastor Tilt sent me here to tell you that you are no longer welcome at *his* church and if you come back to *his* church you will be trespassing."

The "police harassment" was caused by Pastor Tilt, who had a terrible ego/power and evil control issue. It was so evil and wicked that Pastor Tilt came after Prince and Princess' part-time funeral home job where they picked up dead bodies and helped with funeral services. Pastor Tilt told the funeral home director that he would take his church funerals to another funeral home unless he could be assured that Prince and Princess would no longer be used by that funeral home. As a result, Prince and Princess lost their part-time funeral home work. They chose not to bring legal action but instead brought their case to the judge of the universe, God Almighty, and felt led to document their story by way of the pen!

> Now go, write it before them in a table, and note it in a book, that it may be for the time to come for ever and ever:
> That this is a rebellious people, lying children, children that will not hear the law of the Lord:
> Which say to the seers, See not; and to the prophets, Prophesy not unto us right things, speak unto us smooth things, prophesy deceits:
> Get you out of the way, turn aside out of the path, cause the Holy One of Israel to cease from before us.
> Wherefore thus saith the Holy One of Israel, Because ye despise this word, and trust In oppression and perverseness, and stay thereon:
> Therefore this iniquity shall be to you as a breach ready to fall, swelling out in a high wall, whose breaking cometh suddenly at an instant. (Isaiah 30:8–13)

Several people shared with Prince and Princess what they witnessed on Sunday morning, December 16, 2001. The elders stood on guard throughout the whole church service, at all the main entrances to the church. The police were on alert waiting to be called to remove Prince, a seventy-one-year-old minister of the Word of God, and Princess, his sixty-six-year-old wife, who both had given their lives ministering to wounded, hurting, and bleeding sheep. The target of their evil plans, Prince and Princess, did not show up at Pastor Tilt's church; thus, Prince and Princess were not arrested Sunday morning, December 16, 2001, for going to their church, the church they had attended for around five years, the church they attended with their family and friends to worship the Lord.

What a terrible tragedy that citizens of the United States of America must be concerned about maintaining their freedoms. Moral issues of right and wrong have degenerated to an all-time low in America, our beloved country of the free. The church, too often, has become a haven for corruption. And what has been going on for years inside the church world has become part of our government and the political world of today. Pastor Tilt not only controlled his congregation; he also controlled some of the police—at least one policeman who attended his church.

Prince and Princess thought that US churches were inclusive or open to all needy human beings, as the Bible says, "Whosoever will may come," and not exclusive or a secret society where people are under the evil iron-fist rule of their leaders.

Pastor Tilt told Princess, "I have told people before not to come *'to my church,'* and most people have the grace not to come."

Finally, Prince and Princess received a letter from Pastor Tilt and his board, which said, "You are in rebellion against us, the God-ordained, congregation-elected leaders of this church ... We accept sinners in this church, if they confess their sins, repent, make amends, and press on toward biblical obedience. If you wish to be restored into fellowship with us, you must do those things ... until then you are not welcome." This happened because, as Pastor Tilt accused Prince and Princess, "You are lodging with Rad."

When Rad was suffering with severe pain, he found comfort and help from Prince and Princess. Their home became a place of refuge when Rad was on the edge of utter despair. Prince and Princess felt Rad's pain and suffered with him. They opened their arms of love and prayers to him, gave him a haven to flee to, their couch and/or bed to sleep on, food to eat at their table, and gave him their arms of love and comfort, and prayers at a time when Rad so desperately needed help. He was thus rescued from ending his life down at the riverside.

Prince and Princess reached their arms out in love and compassion doing what they had been doing for years, and years, and years, ministering to the needy and binding up their wounds—in obedience to the Lord—and were punished for doing so.

This horrible, diabolical, demonic story of power and control gone evil was almost as tragic as the A/G excommunication, maybe even worse because Prince and Princess were still hurting from the A/G blows and the deep heart-piercing wounds that followed. The evil became more evil when Pastor Tilt was elevated to superintendent of another neighboring district by the very same district officials who backed him in his evil. And likewise, Rocky was elevated to become the secretary/treasurer of the Northwest District—in closer fellowship with his buddies in crime—while at the same time, Pastor Rocky and Pastor Tilt both left behind a trail of wounded and bleeding victims.

God gave Prince and Princess grace and strength to endure the test of faith! Praise the Lord! God enabled them to love their enemies and keep their hearts full of love for the wounded and bleeding. They still loved the Lord; God means everything to them. This tragic story needs to be told, by way of the pen, with a movie following this book, hopefully, in a very productive, interesting, exciting, informative, revealing, and dramatic way—while at the same time bringing glory and honor to God.

Some months later, in June 2003, while Prince and Princess were away from their home for about two weeks, something strange and mysterious was reported to have happened in their home.

Two neighbors declared what they had seen. "Soon after you left home on your vacation with your daughter, Dawn, and her family in Wyoming, Clay and I saw a light go on in your house for about one hour and then off and go on again about two hours later and about one hour later off again," said Beatrice.

"I definitely saw it go on and off three different nights. I documented it. I did not want anybody to think I was imagining things or getting senile, so I asked my wife to walk over to your house in the dark with me where we both looked into your living room window and could easily see everything in the room. The lamp by the window was turned on," Clay declared.

"We were so concerned that I even called the police. They told me that they couldn't do anything about it because they did not have approval from you to break into your house. We did not want to worry you, so we decided to wait until you arrived back home from your vacation," added Beatrice.

It was interesting but a little unnerving to listen to their reports. Prince and Princess decided not to worry about it; they knew their lives belonged to God.

Cecilia, another neighbor, also told Princess, "I saw a man go into your back door and in your backyard." And in addition, two other neighbors told them that they also saw lights go on and off in their house. One of those neighbors said, "I saw a man go into the side door of your garage."

On arriving back home, Princess only noticed one thing out of place in the house. Prince told her, "Do not worry about it. Our lives are in God's hands."

A few days later, something terrible happened to their computer. They called their computer expert, Stash, to their home. After thoroughly checking out the family computer, he helplessly said, "I am very sorry to have to tell you that you have totally lost everything on your computer. It has completely crashed. As a professional computer expert, I do not have any answer for this. I cannot restore anything; it is a complete black screen—a total loss of everything you had on it."

"Oh, that is terrible; I feel sick, and I am very much shocked that this could happen," Princess said. Fortunately, they had the most important information on a backup disc. No doubt, their neighbors did see lights go on and off in the house. Prince and Princess refused to worry about what they were told by their neighbors and continued to trust their lives into God's hands.

Later that evening, Prince and Princess discussed the computer crashing and the neighbors' stories. Prince tried to reassure Princess. "Maybe our neighbors are right. I know that a lot of letters have been mailed back and forth between us and the US Justice Department, including the FBI and IRS. Possibly someone was sent to our house as a spy. Even so, I am going to continue to trust God to take care of us. I know the time is coming when truth and divine justice shall prevail."

Princess also believed that the Lord would continue to take care of them but didn't know what to think about the events they had been told by some of their neighbors. "Wendy thinks the Feds have had us under surveillance. Maybe she is right. You know, honey, Pastor Del told us that George, the US assistant attorney, was thick with Pastor Del Carpe. And George was the US attorney for the Assembly grand jury case—the grand jury case that somehow mysteriously and secretly was dismissed."

"More mysteries!" Prince said. "We must leave this latest mystery with the Lord. He knows who has been in our house, and He knows exactly what happened to our computer. I know God will continue to take care of us. Let us refuse to worry! Praise God for His faithfulness."

"You are right. I will trust in our wonderful Lord to take care of us. I have learned that true righteousness is true justice and true justice is always fair—otherwise there is no justice. Without justice, there is no freedom. When there is no freedom, anarchy reigns. As responsible US citizens, people need to contend for their American heritage—'one nation under God, indivisible, with liberty and justice for all,'" Princess said.

"Remember, Jesus also suffered for exposing sin and evil," Prince added. "Can we expect anything less than He had to endure? The only way to dispel the darkness is to turn on the light. We have only labored to 'turn on the light' by presenting actual and documented material exposing the evil 'elite Mafia' operating within the church. There are those who work to dominate and control everybody and severely punish anyone who dares to question them. Even Good Samaritans who endeavor to help those who are hurting are a target. Truth, in a sense, needs no defense. Truth only needs exposure. It will eventually and always win. As John 17:17 says, 'Sanctify them through thy truth: Thy Word is Truth.' Biblical principles never become outdated. They are ever fresh, ever new, and applicable in any generation, any time. The light of truth is timeless. Nevertheless, fallen humanity, yes, even redeemed humanity, must resist the temptation to compromise and spare wrongful fleshly instincts to prevent exposure of hidden sins. The people whose sins are exposed cry, 'turn off the light!' But God declares, 'turn on the light!'"

Princess couldn't help but smile as she said, "How true! You know, honey, that sounds like another fabulous message waiting for you to preach."

Prince grinned back and continued, "Let us never forget, God loves us; He has kept us and will continue to keep us through all the storms of life. He is our salvation! He will always take care of us! 'Lo, I am with you always.' He has promised, 'I will never leave thee nor forsake thee.' Praise the Lord for His faithfulness to us. Amen!" Princess softly echoed her husband. "Amen!"

Prince gathered his wife in a very loving, tender, close embrace. "I love you more than ever, my sweet darling/precious love. Thank you for being my wife."

Prince continued. "Taking a stand for what is morally just and right, and the resulting cruel and evil blows of retaliation and pain that too often follow, are indescribable—the pain of excommunication from your church family, the loss of your home, the loss of financial income, the pain of even some family members being hurt, and all the misunderstanding that follow are too deep to understand and explain—but, oh, the comfort that comes when we run for help and comfort to the just God of this universe. You can rest assured that He will not despise the broken and contrite heart. As Psalm 147:3 says: 'He healeth the broken in heart, and bindeth up their wounds.' God is the only one who really understands our deep sorrow, pain, and loss."

Both the old and the young feel pain. Prince was never the same after they—his peers and his brethren—got done trying to destroy him and his wife with their evil blows of revenge for exposing some of their corrupt deeds. Prince and Princess were so thankful that they still had each other's love and most of all still had the wonderful love of God in their hearts and lives. Praise the Lord for His wonderful love.

Prince's broken heart went so deep. The buckets of tears shed, daily, on his knees are counted and known only by God. And, of course, his wife, Princess, was never the same either. The hurt and pain was cruel, especially knowing what a man of God her husband was to the very last moment of his life here on earth. How his peers could do this to him, his wife, and their dear/precious children is beyond comprehension. How could they be so cruel, sleep at night, and still call themselves Christians? Prince spent a lot of time praying for their persecutors. Their arms of love and forgiveness remained wide open. Maybe this is one of the reasons why God gave them such sweet peace in their hearts, and why God is so very real and precious to them and their children and grandchildren. They love the Lord so very much. Praise His wonderful name, the precious name of Jesus.

A passage from the foreword of the book *White Collar Crime in the Church*, written by Lynn Franklin, follows:

> What is love, compassion, and holiness? These are all attributes that God wants us to have. What is God's plan? Is it just taking care of me, my family, and, as a pastor, my congregation?
>
> I was raised in a God-fearing Christian home. I do not remember any time that God was not a part of the daily conversation. As a little girl, I went to sleep listening to my dad read the Bible out loud. Early in life I was taught about love, compassion, holiness, and a fear of the Lord. God not only loved ME but God also expected something from me. He expected my obedience and to stand in AWE of HIM.
>
> Today, too many pastors are so caught up in their leadership and their congregations lining up with their authority, which they believe is a direct line from God, that living with integrity or being beyond

reproach is left behind. Where is the standing up for what is right? As one pastor told me, "you have to pick your battles." These battles, more and more, seem to be about proving who the leader is and not about God. Through the years, I've watched my Dad let God have control instead of trying to prove to others who was the leader. All through my growing up years, getting up at 5:00 a.m. or earlier to get ready for school, my Dad would already be up. He was sitting at the table reading his Bible or on his knees. More times than I could even count, I would see my parents in their room on their knees praying and crying out to God. What a wonderful blessing I grew up with; although, I did not realize this till later in life.

Where is the "Old Rugged Cross" in our lives? Where are the bond servants of Jesus Christ/chains of the gospel, as Paul speaks of in Philemon 1:13, "Ministered unto me in the bonds of the gospel:" Consider Joseph, who was sent as a slave to Egypt by his brothers; yet refusing to sin to save himself and keep his position. "Because thou art his wife: how then can I do this great wickedness, and sin against God?" (Genesis 39:9) As a result of his desire to do what God wanted, he was thrown into prison. Joseph was eventually elevated to a high position of leadership. Why? Because he was faithful; he never lost his hope or faith in his God. Can the church and pastors give up their name for truth and righteousness?

It seems, more and more, what the church holds close to their heart is a self-inflated holiness. Is this what God holds dear? No, it is a holy and righteous life and to expose sin for what it is. This is what is dear to Prince and Princess' hearts no matter the outcome to their lives. In my darkest times, they have been there to encourage me and most of all pray. I have much faith in God and His Word because of my parents. In their darkest times, they have stood firm in their faith. I have watched my parents, Prince and Princess, lose their pastorate, fellowship with other pastors, and "a name" because of their integrity! They would rather lose all this world has to offer than disobey God. What they have done is stand for truth, God's truth! Where are their former peers? They are hiding their sin, covering it up.

Yes, it is easier to hide than to expose. Yes, it is easier to pick the battles of less consequence to your life. Esther is also someone who had a desire to do what God wanted her to do and was willing to take the consequences that would come to her. "I also and my maidens will fast likewise; and so will I go in unto the king, which is not according to the law: and if I perish, I perish" (Esther 4:16b). Esther knew she needed to go before the king and inform him about Haman's plot to kill the Jews. She also knew that to do this could bring her death. Esther knew that she needed to obey God even if she lost her life. Just like Esther, the battles we fight aren't always our sin or our personal battles. Sometimes God asks us to fight battles for others even if we lose what this world holds dear. Prince and Princess, my Mom and Dad, have had much taken from them, however, they have gained much more by God's standards. This is what we all should ultimately desire and strive for.

There are still a lot of wonderful godly Christian sheep and pastors left in the different church denominations, who really love God and are trying to spread the wonderful gospel of our Lord Jesus Christ. We personally know some of them. They do not know where else to go or what to do.

May God send a spiritual awakening to all the church

denominations in the world before it is too late. This is the end-time falling away. It is the spiritual sifting time. Those who love God will have to determine in their minds and hearts to remain faithful and true to the Lord during this terrible end-time deception.

God's love and forgiveness is given to all who will come to Him.

> Now go, write it before them in a table, and note it in a book, that it may be for the time to come for ever and ever:
>
> That this is a rebellious people, lying children, children that will not hear the law of the Lord:
>
> Which say to the seers, See not; and to the prophets, Prophesy not unto us right things, speak unto us smooth things, prophesy deceits:
>
> Get you out of the way, turn aside out of the path, cause the Holy One of Israel to cease from before us.
>
> Wherefore thus saith the Holy One of Israel, Because ye despise this word, and trust In oppression and perverseness, and stay thereon:
>
> Therefore this iniquity shall be to you as a breach ready to fall, swelling out in a high wall, whose breaking cometh suddenly at an instant. (Isaiah 30:8–13)

Prince and Princess sat discussing how the "backsliding" church was and is an enormous influence on the US government.

"I thought the churches in the United States of America were inclusive or open to all needy human beings, as the Bible says, "Whosoever will may come," and not exclusive or a secret society where people are under the evil iron-fist rule of their leaders," said Princess.

"What a terrible tragedy that the citizens of the United States of America have to be concerned about maintaining their freedoms. Moral issues of right and wrong have degenerated to an all-time low in America, our beloved country of the free. The church, too often, has become a haven for corruption. And what has been going on for years inside the church world has become part of our government and the political world of today," responded Prince.

"We will continue to trust God to take care of us. I have learned that true righteousness is true justice, and true justice is always fair; otherwise, there is no justice. Without justice, there is no freedom. When there is no freedom, anarchy reigns. As responsible US citizens, people need to contend for their American heritage—one nation under God, indivisible, with liberty and justice for all," said Princess.

"Remember, Jesus also suffered for exposing sin and evil," Prince said. "Can we expect anything less than He had to endure? The only way to dispel the darkness is to turn on the light. We have only labored to 'turn on the light' by presenting actual and documented material exposing the evil 'elite Mafia' operating within the church. There are those who work to dominate and control everybody and severely punish anyone who dares to question them—even Good Samaritans who endeavor to help those who are hurting are a target. Truth, in a sense, needs no defense. Truth only needs exposure. It will eventually and always win. As John 17:17 says: 'Sanctify them through thy truth: Thy Word is Truth.' Biblical principles never become outdated. They are ever fresh, ever new, and applicable in any generation, any time. The light of truth is timeless. Nevertheless, fallen humanity, yes, even redeemed humanity, must resist the temptation to compromise and spare wrongful fleshly instincts to prevent exposure of hidden sins. The people whose sins are exposed cry, 'turn off the light!' But God declares, 'turn on the light!'"

Princess couldn't help but smile as she said, "How true! You know, honey, that sounds like another fabulous message waiting for you to preach." (They stole Prince's pastorate church ministry from him and ordered him to be "quiet," but they couldn't stop him from continuing to preach the Word of God, and ministering to hungry and and/or needy souls.)

Prince grinned back and continued, "Let us never forget, God loves us; He has kept us, and will continue to keep us through all the storms of life. He is our salvation! He will always take care of us! 'Lo, I am with you always,' He has promised, 'I will never leave thee nor forsake thee.' Praise the Lord for His faithfulness to us. Amen!" Princess softly echoed her husband, "Amen!"

Prince gathered his wife in a very loving, tender, close embrace, "I love you more than ever, my sweet darling / precious love. Thank you for being my wife."

Prince continued, "Taking a stand for what is morally just and right and the resulting cruel and evil blows of retaliation and pain that too often follow, are indescribable—the pain of excommunication from your church family, the loss of your public pastorate, the loss of your home, the loss of financial income, the pain of even some 'dear' family members being hurt, and all the misunderstanding that follow are too deep to understand and explain—but, oh, the comfort that comes when we run for help and comfort to the just God of this Universe. You can rest assured that 'He will not despise the broken and contrite heart.' 'He healeth the broken in heart and bindeth up their wounds.' (Psalm 147:3) God is the only one who really understands our deep sorrow, pain, and loss."

They couldn't silence him when he was exposing their corruption. When they took his pastorate (church platform ministry) away from him, they couldn't silence him or stop him from exposing their church corruption, and they couldn't silence him or stop him from preaching the Word of God, proclaiming the gospel to "whosoever," in senior retirement centers, rest homes, in books, (movies) and wherever they found a place to minister, and, of course, without any salary. He even preached the gospel on his death bed. One night, our daughter, Dawn, said that she heard him on the baby monitor (that they had set up to help keep him safe) preach a whole sermon out loud, with even an altar call, in the middle of the night, while in his hospital bed in the kitchen, just like he did while he was pastoring." When they excommunicated him and took his pastorate away, we were marked people, they made sure of that! Prince's name was put on the "scandal sheet"—the "blacklist." But, praise God, Prince's name was/is written in the Heavenly Book, as one of the "Redeemed Saints" of God.

For some needed extra income, Prince started working at the local grocery store. I felt so bad for my husband, he was so sweet about it all, even when he had to get down on his knees on the store floor and clean up the glass and what spilled out of the broken bottles, such as milk or wine. He would help sack groceries and go out in very cold snowy weather, helping customers, and then bring back in the grocery carts. Then he would come home with his small paycheck and hand it to me with a big, sweet smile. He loved me, dearly, so very much—My heart ached for him, and I loved him dearly, so very much, more than ever! On his knees on the store floor cleaning up the messes, and while pushing grocery carts in the cold snowy below zero weather, he continued to pray and praise the Lord!

Both the old and the young feel pain. Prince was never the same, after they, his peers and his brethren, got done trying to destroy him and his wife with their evil blows of revenge for 'whistle blowing,' exposing some of their corrupt deeds. Prince and Princess were so thankful that they still had each other's love and most of all still had the wonderful love of God in their hearts and lives. Praise the Lord for His Wonderful Love."

Prince's broken heart went so deep! God says in His Word, "God will not despise a *broken heart.*" The buckets of tears shed, daily, on his knees are counted and known only by God. And, of course, his wife, Princess, was never the same either, the hurt and pain was cruel, especially knowing what a man of God her husband was to the very last moment of his life here on earth. How could his peers do this to him, his wife, and their dear/precious children, is beyond comprehension. How could they be so cruel, sleep at night, and still call themselves Christians. Prince spent a lot of time praying for their persecutors. Their arms of love and forgiveness remained wide open. Maybe, this is one of the reasons why God gave them such sweet peace in their hearts, and why God is so very real and precious to them and their children and grandchildren. They love the Lord so very much. Praise His wonderful name, the precious name of Jesus.

There are still a lot of wonderful godly Christian sheep and pastors left, who really love God and are trying to spread the wonderful gospel of our Lord Jesus Christ. We personally know some of them. They do not know where else to go or what to do. May God send a spiritual awakening to all the church denominations in the world before it is too late. This is the end-time falling away. It is the spiritual sifting time. Those who love God will have to determine in their minds and hearts to remain faithful and true to the Lord during this terrible end-time deception. God's love and forgiveness is given to all who will come to him.

Prince shares from his heart some things. "All of our pastorates were conservative? Yes, especially by today's standards, we are/were definitely considered conservative.

"The average age and background of those attending was a mixed-age attendance. Of course, as our six children grew older, other young people were attracted. We have had farmers, professional people of all occupations, educated and uneducated, civil (sheriff's deputy), police, teachers, nurses, etc.—just a cross section of humanity.

> I delight to do thy will, O my God: yea, thy law is within my heart.
>
> I have preached righteousness in the great congregation: lo, I have not reframed my lips, O Lord, thou knowest.
>
> I have not hid thy righteousness within my heart; I have declared thy faithfulness and thy salvation: I have not concealed thy loving-kindness and thy truth from the great congregation." (Psalm 40:8–10)

Prince shares, "Our goal and passion, which has only become stronger over the years, was and has been to first of all be loyal to God and obedient to Him, whatever the cost. Therefore, I understood in any situation that my loyalty to the Assemblies of God took second place after my loyalty to the living God and my wife and family. I would probably be classed as a maverick.

"I wasn't a 'good ol' boy' because; my wife and family came first, after God. Thus, I did not have time to fraternize with the 'powers that be.' I was very much a family man; very devoted to my wife and six children. We went shopping with our six children, traveling, vacations together with them in harvest while I drove pea/ wheat combines in Walla Walla, zoos, in short, just being together as a family. We did everything we could with our six children, even taking them with us to District and General Council when at all possible. We did not often eat "out" simply because of cost. I guess our hobbies were just being together as a family; food canning, gardening, making apple cider, Princess teaching our daughters sewing, music, holding musical concerts as a family, and me doing paper routes with my sons and playing baseball with them. Our whole family has been involved in music through the years. We traveled to other churches and gave one-hour music concerts. It was a wonderful time in our lives.

"I never in my own heart considered myself an 'outsider'; there simply were some priorities that were more important than district directives. However, I believe I had the respect of my ministering brethren and leaders. I was able to call the district at any time and talk to the leaders on a first-name basis. Years ago in the beginning of our ministry, the older leaders we called "Brother ...."

Princess shares, "We considered ourselves as coleaders, per Prince's request when we first started pastoring.

Prince shares, "From early in our marriage we (Princess and I) worked together even while endeavoring to be faithful parents to our six children. It was often very difficult balancing family and church responsibilities. But we did the best we knew how given the circumstances."

Prince shares, "After the murders of our church friends (told in detail in Princess' book *Broken, Yet Triumphant*, the church split; we then started a new church without Assemblies of God Northwest District approval. (Years later, praise the Lord, the movie *A Murder of Innocence* was produced based on the book). We were severely punished and rebuked for starting a church (Olympic Gospel Tabernacle) without the Assemblies of God Northwest District officials' approval. As punishment, I was not allowed to minister— for one year—in an Assemblies of God church other than our home church, which was also Assemblies of God. We were allowed to minister in other churches, as well.

"In addition to the church that split, there were some power struggles as, at least to us, it was the most 'worldly' church we had ever pastored. Immorality was not one isolated case—incest, sex perversion, etc. In Princess' book *Broken, Yet Triumphant,* she tells about the instance where a deacon from the church that split followed us in starting another church. Soon, thereafter, he was discovered in immorality with another man's wife. When I (Pastor Prince) found out about it, I confronted him and was promised his sin was in the past, never to be repeated. We thought that episode was over. Sadly, his indiscretion continued. Apparently, he wanted to get the attention off himself and his immoral conduct and started falsely accusing my wife of being a troublemaker. Thus, when I discovered this and his continued immorality, I told my wife, "I am sick and tired of digging around in the cesspool of iniquity," and resigned the new church that we had so recently organized and started and moved on to a new ministry."

Princess shares, "We (Prince and I) never believed in holding grudges against anyone. If we let the disappointments, trials, and tests of life make us bitter instead of better we only destroy ourselves. I know that many of the physical ailments that people have come from unforgiveness, resentment, hatred, and envy in the heart, and, of course, at the same time, some come from stress and/or a broken heart, and/or old age, poor health, accidents, and/or for different other reasons.

"Taking a stand for what is morally just and right, at times, can be very painful. But we can rest assured that 'He will not despise the broken and contrite heart.' 'He healeth the broken in heart, and bindeth up their wounds' (Psalm 147:3). God is the only one who really understands our deep sorrow, pain, and/or loss. Both the old and the young feel pain.

"I am thankful to God for giving Prince and me such sweet peace in our hearts; God has always been so very real and precious to us and our family. I am so grateful and thankful to the Lord for blessing our family with such a wonderful, beautiful, God-honoring funeral celebration, on March 16, 2013, which was seven days after (March 9, 2013) when the angel of the Lord came and ushered Prince into his royal heavenly home, to forever be with his wonderful Lord, Savior, and Heavenly Father, forever safe and free of pain and suffering. 'Thank you, Jesus!' We love the Lord so very much. Praise His wonderful name, the precious name of Jesus.

"The Lord is my light and my salvation; whom shall I fear? The Lord is the strength of my life; of whom shall I be afraid?

"There are still a lot of wonderful godly Christian sheep and pastors, who really love God and are trying to spread the wonderful gospel of our Lord Jesus Christ. May God send a spiritual awakening to any and all of the ungodly church pastors and/or church leaders in any and all of the church denominations before it is too late. This is the time of the end-time falling away—the spiritual sifting time. Those who love God will have to determine in their minds and hearts to remain faithful and true to the Lord during this terrible end-time deception.

"Medical research is finding out that the biblical statement, 'A merry heart doeth good like a medicine,' is indeed a true statement (Proverbs 17:22).

"We can let the tests and trials of life either make us bitter or better. The 'I' makes the difference. Are we going to be selfish and put *I* on the throne all the time or are we going to bless others with love, kindness, and forgiveness?

"We can determine to make this a better world to live in.

"One year during our Christmas program, we gave everyone a small candle, turned out the lights, and all the small candles together lit up the big church. So we can all be little lights shining in our part of this big, dark world.

"Believe me, God hasn't forgotten you! Or me! You are important, this is proven by the fact Jesus Christ died for you.

"We have determined, with God's help, to make this a more beautiful world to live in by living an overcoming triumphant life.

"I grew up living on a wheat farm in Walla Walla, Washington. I know from experience that how many machinery breakdowns in harvest is not the most important thing, but do we bring in the harvest, do we finish bringing in the grain before the winter rains come and spoil the grain?

"Often, we are tested with various kinds of trials in this world. It is not the most important thing how many times we fall, sin, or fail God in some way, but do we get up and press on to glorious triumphant victory.

"A few days after Prince's mother died, Prince and I made a rush trip for a brief visit with Prince's only brother, Given, and his wife, Arlene. On our way back home, we feasted on some delicious oranges while driving in the car. We didn't have time to make dinner and arrive at the church on time for me to conduct the church "Christmas" program practice. Thus, we quickly ate more oranges, and again after the practice the oranges still looked good enough to eat. I think too much stress, too many oranges, and drinking too much water at one time threw my body off, and I became extremely sick with kidney infection and water intoxication.

"When I started to fade out of this world, my dear husband carried me to the car and took me to the emergency room of the hospital where I was unconscious for about thirty hours. My husband, Prince, our children, other family members, and many friends prayed me through to health again. Praise be to God for His healing touch in our daily lives. We can determine to be triumphant no matter the test. We are winners through Jesus Christ our Lord and Savior!

The following 1990 Christmas letter gives more details.

> Prince shares,
> Christmas—1990
> Dear family and friends:
>
> "Thanks be unto God for his unspeakable [priceless] gift" (11 Corinthians 9:15). At this season we have great cause for giving abundant thanks and praise to our God. Consider then …

"First, thanks to our wonderful Heavenly Father for the "priceless" gift of His Son, *Jesus*! "For unto you is born this day in the city of David a Saviour, which is Christ the Lord" (Luke 2:11). *Jesus* is our only hope, and without Him there is no salvation. He is always faithful and has promised never to leave those who put their trust in Him. "We love him, because he first loved us" (1 John 4:19).

"Second, we are so very *thankful* that God graciously spared my wife's life ten days ago. On Thursday, December 13, shortly before 5:00 p.m., I carried my wife from our bedroom to the car and rushed to the local hospital emergency room. Though Princess was apparently awake (eyes open), she made no response to my earnest pleas to speak to me. In the emergency room, tests were begun. It was discovered that the 'sodium serum' level in her blood had dropped so quickly that it produced a neurological 'shock' to her system making it impossible for her to communicate. Along with this, at the same time she had developed a serious kidney infection, which also produced a 'shock' to her body.

"People across the states of Washington, Oregon, and Idaho were alerted, and believing prayer began ascending to Heaven. Oh, how wonderful to belong to the 'family of God,' especially in a time of urgent need! While we appreciate everything medical science did for my wife, we are persuaded that it was *God* who so graciously healed Princess' body, in answer to the prayers of His people. She suddenly awakened about 4:15 p.m., Friday, December 14, and began asking questions (the first time in more than twenty-four hours). 'What's going on?' 'Where am I?' 'How did I get here?' (Wonderful words!) She just could not understand why she needed all the tubes and wires connected to her body. Not only was she unable to communicate for more than twenty-four hours, but she also suffered 'total global amnesia' for a period of about thirty hours. The doctor said she will never recall those hours, but then, with the pain and suffering, that's probably a blessing—for she remembers none of it. About 4:30 p.m. on Saturday, December 15, Princess was discharged from the hospital, and sent home to regain her strength.

"Third, we cannot thank *you* enough ... our church family here in Ellensburg, for your outpouring of love and compassion to my wife, to me, and to our children in this time of urgent need. Your prayers, love and concern, cards, and kind support have touched our hearts and will never be forgotten! Also, our thanks to *all* the people who prayed all over the Northwest. Thanks, also, to the church board for giving us four weeks' sick leave for rest and recuperation. We love you, everyone, and pray God's richest blessing upon you! Surely, nothing *just happens*, therefore we claim Romans 8:28: 'And we know that all things work together for good to them that love God, to them who are the called according to his purpose.'

"With much love, appreciation, and prayers,"

Pastor Prince
Prince and Princess
Mark and Jonathan

When Prince was excommunicated from the AG and CMA churches, Jonathan, Dawn, Larry, and I were all cast out with him. Jonathan and Dawn and I were all unpaid assistant pastors to Prince. Jonathan led the music and worship service, taught Sunday school, drove the church van to pick up children for Sunday school, helped clean the church, and helped wherever he was needed by his dad and mom. Dawn played the piano, sang special songs, led the choir, worked in children's church, plus wherever needed by her dad and mom. Larry ran the sound system, was a board member, and helped wherever needed. I was the Sunday school superintendent for years, the Kids Krusade director, played the piano when Dawn played the organ, sang music specials with Prince and family, and helped wherever I was needed in the church. Sometimes even preached. And, of course, this excommunication from both churches severely affected our whole family, including our grandchildren.

God's love for Prince and Princess and our family and our love for God was *triumphant*—love and forgiveness reigned and brought sweet peace into our hearts and lives. We were victorious with God's help. I would like for this message somehow to be given in our second, forthcoming movie.

Larry and Dawn took Prince and me and Jonathan for a few days visit at Larry's parents' home in Riggins, Idaho, to try and help us in our deep sorrow and hurt. We visited the salmon fish hatchery. Also, they took us camping. And a Minister friend and his wife took us on a tour of Israel. This all helped, but the pain and wounds were still there. I am so thankful that through it all, we always felt the sweet abiding love and presence of our wonderful Lord and Savior, Jesus Christ.

Without question, any level of Christian leadership is an awesome responsibility. Failure here produces waves of destructive influence that cannot be measured. The "called" ministry, whether pastoral or strictly executive and administrative, deals in the currency of eternal souls. Thus, a spiritual yet practical idealism must guide all leaders in their sphere of ministry. Apostle Paul states this succinctly in 2 Corinthians 6:3 when he says: "Giving no offence in anything, that the ministry be not blamed."

While every Christian's life is an open letter, "known and read of all men," any appointed or elected position of church leadership carries with it an additional weight of accountability and responsibility. It is here that godly standards of practical righteousness must come under even closer scrutiny, in part because of the potential influence and high visibility. Even greater must be the understanding that it is the living, eternal, and infinitely holy God Who is being served; and He is the judge, not finite man. It is before the eyes of a largely unbelieving and Christ-rejecting world that we live our lives. Many look for flaws in professing Christians (especially leaders) to bolster their reasons for rejecting the gospel, and, at the same time, they find another opportunity to blaspheme God.

This is aptly illustrated in the Old Testament. It was Nathan, the prophet, who said to King David, following his sins of adultery, murder, and lying (2 Samuel 12:14), "by this deed thou hast given great occasion to the enemies of the Lord to blaspheme." David's kingly position, influence, and visibility only compounded the awful effects of his sin. Though forgiven, he reaped the bitter results of those sins the rest of his life. The question may be asked: Has the dispensation of grace diluted or changed this principle? Certainly not, for it is Paul, in writing to Christians, who exhorts, "Be not deceived; God is not mocked: for whatsoever a man soweth, that shall he also reap" (Galatians 6:7). Again, the destructive influence upon other souls cannot be calculated.

There is no joy in exposing sin and wrongdoing, but silence only allows the leaven of corruption to spread. No doubt, the camp will be divided. Some will defend those exposed in their sin; others will rejoice that wrong is uncovered. Jesus said, "For there is nothing covered, that shall not be revealed, neither hid, that shall not be known" (Luke 12:2).

The biblical purpose for making sin known is for redemption, so that those involved in wrongdoing may be corrected and their sin judged, as well as serving to warn others to walk a higher road.

Every effort has been made to be factual. Firsthand witness and certified documentation substantiate the story told. This account centers around the search for truth and righteousness, which must prevail at all levels in the Body of Christ. There must be *one* standard for laity and leadership. If something is wrong for the person in the pew, then it is equally wrong for the one in leadership. If we are to be successful in winning souls to Christ, one requirement is essential: there must be consistency between the doctrines we teach and preach and the walk we walk. If we talk the talk, we must walk the walk. This should be with no difference between laity and leadership. The world has little defense against purity of doctrine lived out in practical and holy living. We may be ever so correct in doctrine, but without application of truth in everyday living, our teaching is worthless—yes, even destructive. Perhaps Paul summed it up in revealing his own passion: "And herein do I exercise myself, to have always a conscience void of offence toward God, and toward men" (Acts 24:16).

Again, it was Paul who exhorted, "Examine yourselves, whether ye be in the faith; prove your own selves" (2 Corinthians 13:5). Surely, we as believers need often to examine ourselves, both as to acceptance of truth and our display of the same. Therefore, read this book, not to condemn a person, but with the heart cry, "Search *me*, O God, and know *my* heart: try *me*, and know *my* thoughts: And see if there be any wicked way in *me*, and lead *me* in the way everlasting" (Psalm 139:23–24). (Writer's emphasis.)

We are all pilgrims; we have not arrived. No person is an island to himself. We need at times the rebuke of a brother. Sin needs to be confronted. Eternity is too long to assume all is well if indeed it is not. Better to be ashamed *now* where remedy is possible than to stand ashamed before God in eternity when no recourse is granted.

To laity and leader alike then … read on, knowing that "… every one of us shall give an account of himself to God" (Romans 14:12).

Our daughter, Lynn, wrote in her foreword the following:

> It seems, more and more, what the church holds close to their heart is a self-inflated holiness. Is this what God holds dear? No, it is a holy and righteous life and to expose sin for what it is. This is what is dear to Prince and Princess' hearts no matter the outcome to their lives. In my darkest times they have been there to encourage me and most of all pray. I have much

faith in God and His Word because of my parents. In their darkest times they have stood firm in their faith. I have watched my parents, Prince and Princess, lose their pastorate, fellowship with other pastors, and "a name" because of their integrity! They would rather lose all this world has to offer than disobey God. What they have done is stand for truth, God's truth! Where are their former peers? They are hiding their sin, covering it up. Yes, it is easier to hide than to expose. Yes, it is easier to pick the battles of less consequence to your life. Esther is also someone who had a desire to do what God wanted her to do and was willing to take the consequences that would come to her. "I also and my maidens will fast likewise; and so will I go in unto the king, which is not according to the law: and if I perish, I perish" (Esther 4:16b). Esther knew she needed to go before the king and inform him about Haman's plot to kill the Jews. She also knew that to do this could bring her death. Esther knew that she needed to obey God even if she lost her life. Just like Esther, the battles we fight aren't always our sin or our personal battles. Sometimes God asks us to fight battles for others even if we lose what this world holds dear. Prince and Princess, my Mom and Dad, have had much taken from them, however, they have gained much more by God's standards. This is what we all should ultimately desire and strive for.

Those who question established authority can be trampled on, crushed, thrown aside, and shunned while at the same time "Moral Values" are all mixed up and of no value. Yet, from the hearts of those who truly pant after God and His Righteousness comes an urgent/impassioned "Cry for Moral Values." "As the hart panteth after the water brooks, so panteth my soul after thee, O God" (Psalm 42:1).

The great mysterious secrecy surrounding the "QUESTIONABLE" grand jury investigation helped hide the U.S. attorney conflict of interest. The American grand jury system can be good but we have discovered that it also can be very dangerous to justice because of all the secrecy; which enables potential miscarriage of justice at the highest levels of government. At all levels of the Church and Government there has been cover-up and more cover-up of the cover-up. The Grand Jury secrecy/mystery has greatly helped to conceal the corruption, and the corrupt cover-up of the corruption. For years, the Federal agents and Church Officials carried on with their big ruse.

We have found the Lord to be our source of strength while refusing to surrender to the "severe evil threats" that have come against us personally from both Church and Civil Authority. Thus, because of the gravity of this unbelievable (somewhat repetitive) story, we continue to share it with you, the public, in this book which is based on a true story.

At times, the truth can be very painful to hear and even more difficult to resolve. It is hypocritical for church leaders to use the church as a safe sanctuary from civil prosecution when committing ungodly and illegal acts that God condemns in His Word; the Word of God that those same church leaders preach and teach. Moreover, if Civil Government officials have family roots in that same church organization it is difficult if not impossible to do justice because of the strong conflict of interest. "To do justice and judgment is more acceptable to the Lord than sacrifice" (Proverbs 21:3).

We are witnessing the great end-time deception that the Bible prophesies will take place in the last days, "Right is wrong and wrong is right." GRAND

JURY MYSTERY turns a spotlight on the crisis of church integrity, as well as "spiritual wickedness in high places," including both the Church Officiary and the United States Justice System. Despite this, there is still hope and help for all in the Lord. One of these ordinary days, the mysterious ongoing miscarriage of justice and intrigue in the church leadership and the legal system of this world will be done away with.

When arrogant and rebellious church leaders refuse to listen and heed the messengers of righteousness that God appoints to expose or reveal gross pharisaical sins, eventually God's judgment will fall. Refusal to receive God's correction through whomever God sends will finally cause the Holy Spirit to withdraw from those who are rejecting His message. Soon Jesus Christ will appear on the scene and righteous judgment will be meted out. Truth and Divine Justice shall prevail! "Shall not the Judge of all the earth do right?" (Genesis 18:25).

Righteousness is true Justice and True Justice is always fair—otherwise there is no Justice. Without Justice, there is no Freedom. When there is no freedom, anarchy reigns. As responsible United States citizens, let us contend for our American heritage before we lose it completely—"One Nation under God, Indivisible, with Liberty and Justice for all."

The Lord is my light and my salvation; whom shall I fear? The Lord is the strength of my life; of whom shall I be afraid? When the wicked, even mine enemies and my foes, came upon me to eat up my flesh, they stumbled and fell. One thing have I desired of the Lord, that will I seek after; that I may dwell in the house of the Lord all the days of my life, to behold the beauty of the Lord, and to inquire in his temple. (Psalm 27:1–2, 4)

The elders stood on guard throughout the whole church service, at all the main entrances to the church. The police were on alert waiting to be called to remove Prince, a seventy-one-year-old minister of the Word of God and Princess, his sixty-six-year-old wife, who both had given their lives ministering to wounded, hurting, and bleeding sheep. The target of their evil plans, Prince and Princess, did not show up at Pastor Tilt's church; thus, Prince and Princess were not arrested Sunday morning, December 16, 2001, for going to their church, the church they had attended for around five years, the church they attended with their family and friends to worship the Lord.

What a terrible tragedy that citizens of the United States of America must be concerned about maintaining their freedoms. Moral issues of right and wrong have degenerated to an all-time low in America, our beloved country of the free. The church, too often, has become a haven for corruption. And what has been going on for years inside the church world has become part of our government, and the political world of today. Pastor Tilt not only held control over his congregation; he also held control over some of the police, at least one policeman who attended his church.

Prince and Princess thought that the churches in the United States of America were inclusive or open to all needy human beings, as the Bible says, "Whosoever will may come," and not exclusive or a secret society where people are under the evil iron-fist rule of their leaders.

Pastor Tilt told Princess, "I have told people before not to come *to my church,* and most people have the grace not to come."

Finally, Prince and Princess received a letter from Pastor Tilt and his board, which said, "You are in rebellion against us, the God-ordained, congregation-elected leaders of this church … We accept sinners in this church, if they confess their sins, repent, make amends, and press on toward biblical obedience. If you wish to be restored into fellowship with us, you must do those things … until then you are not welcome." This happened, all because, as Pastor Tilt accused Prince and Princess, "You are lodging with Rad."

When Rad was really suffering with severe pain, he found comfort and help from Prince and Princess. Their home became a place of refuge when Rad was on the edge of utter despair. Prince and Princess felt Rad's pain and suffered with him. They opened their arms of love and prayers to him, gave him a haven to flee to, their couch and/or bed to sleep on, food to eat at their table, and gave him their arms of love and comfort, and prayers, at a time when Rad so desperately needed help. He was thus rescued from ending his life down at the riverside. Prince and Princess reached their arms out in love and compassion, doing what they had been doing for years, and years, and years, ministering to the needy and binding up their wounds—in obedience to the Lord—and were punished for doing so.

This horrible, diabolical, demonic, story of power and control gone evil was almost as tragic as the A/G excommunication, maybe even worse because Prince and Princess were still hurting from the A/G blows and the deep heart-piercing wounds that followed. The evil became more evil when Pastor Tilt was elevated to superintendent of another neighboring district by the very same district officials who backed him in his evil. And likewise, Rocky was elevated to become the secretary/treasurer of the Northwest District—in closer fellowship with his buddies in crime—while at the same time, Pastor Rocky and Pastor Tilt both left behind a trail of wounded and bleeding victims.

God gave Prince and Princess grace and strength to endure the test of faith! Praise the Lord! God enabled them to love their enemies and keep their hearts full of love for the wounded and bleeding. They still loved the Lord; God means everything to them. This tragic story needs to be told, by way of the pen with a movie following this book, hopefully, in a very productive, interesting, exciting, informative, revealing, and dramatic way—while at the same time bringing glory and honor to God.

"We will trust in our wonderful Lord to take care of us. I have learned that true righteousness is true justice, and true justice is always fair—otherwise there is no justice. Without justice, there is no freedom. When there is no freedom, anarchy reigns. As responsible United States citizens, people need to contend for their American heritage—one nation under God, indivisible, with liberty and justice for all," said Princess.

"Remember, Jesus also suffered for exposing sin and evil. Can we expect anything less than He had to endure? The only way to dispel the darkness is to turn on the light. We have only labored to 'turn on the light' by presenting actual and documented material exposing the evil elite Mafia operating within the church. Some work to dominate and control everybody and severely punish anyone who dares to question them. Even Good Samaritans, who endeavor to help those who are hurting, are a target. Truth, in a sense, needs no defense. Truth only needs exposure. It will eventually and always win. 'Sanctify them through thy truth: Thy Word is Truth' (John 17:17). Biblical principles never become outdated. They are ever fresh, ever new, and applicable in any generation, any time. The light of truth is timeless. Nevertheless, fallen humanity, yes, even redeemed humanity, must resist the temptation to compromise and spare wrongful fleshly instincts to prevent exposure of hidden sins. The people whose sins are exposed cry, 'turn off the light!' But God declares, 'turn on the light!'"

Princess couldn't help but smile as she said, "How true! You know, honey, that sounds like another fabulous message waiting for you to preach."

Prince grinned back and continued, "Let us never forget, God loves us; He has kept us, and will continue to keep us through all the storms of life. He is our salvation! He will always take care of us! 'Lo, I am with you always,' He has promised, 'I will never leave thee nor forsake thee.' Praise the Lord for His faithfulness to us. Amen!"

Princess softly echoed her husband. "Amen!"

Prince gathered his wife in a very loving, tender, close embrace, "I love you more than ever, my sweet darling/precious love. Thank you for being my wife."

Prince continued. "Taking a stand for what is morally just and right and the resulting cruel and evil blows of retaliation and pain that too often follow are indescribable—the pain of excommunication from your church family, the loss of your home, the loss of financial income, the pain of even some family members being hurt, and all the misunderstanding that follow are too deep to understand and explain;

but, oh, the comfort that comes when we run for help and comfort to the just God of this universe. You can rest assured that "He will not despise the broken and contrite heart." "He healeth the broken in heart, and bindeth up their wounds" (Psalm 147:3). God is the only one who really understands our deep sorrow, pain, and loss."

Both the old and the young feel pain. Prince and Princess were so thankful that they still had each other's love and most of all still had the wonderful love of God in their hearts and lives. Praise the Lord for His Wonderful Love." Their arms of love and forgiveness remained wide open. Maybe, this is one of the reasons why God gave them such sweet peace in their hearts, and why God is so very real and precious to them and their children and grandchildren. They love the Lord so very much. Praise His Wonderful Name, the Precious Name of Jesus.

This is the end-time falling away. It is the spiritual sifting time. Those who love God will have to determine in their minds and hearts to remain faithful and true to the Lord during this terrible end-time deception. God's love and forgiveness is given to all who will come to him.

A divine principle prevails. Victory in one test only prepares us for future assignments, which are more difficult. This is the way it is in school—when the students pass one test, they go on to higher, more difficult tests. In the very beginning, God created male and female with a mind that remembers the lessons learned in life's schoolroom.

Sometimes, Princess wondered why she was inspired to write her book *Broken, Yet Triumphant*, because of all the problems that followed that book. Then, years later, the movie *A Murder of Innocence* was produced based on that very same book. This book and the movie, bathed in so much prayer, has been a blessing and continues to be a blessing to many lives. Praise and thanks be to our wonderful Lord and Savior, Jesus Christ.

Long ago, Princess chose to allow God to lead her according to His infinite wisdom and perfect plan. She has determined, with the help and grace of God, to pass the tests that God brings into her life. Sometimes those tests have been difficult and hard to understand.

Princess turned to Prince and asked, "Why did I write that first book? Look at all the problems we have had since it was published. *Broken Yet Triumphant*—huh, I do not feel very triumphant right now. I feel like throwing it in the ocean or burning it. What good is it? Look at all the problems I had getting it back from the publishing company, and all the heartache and grief in my family since it came out, as well as the rejection of the book and myself by some of our own church officials. Reverend Mar Borough and his close associate, Reverend Ransom, in my opinion, have used their power to influence some of the key church officials to reject the book. I believe they have behaved that way because they are not too happy with how the book revealed them to be. Sometimes I wish you would share with them how you feel about it. You've expressed to me, as well as others, that you feel the book could be a real blessing to them if they didn't take it so personally ... Oh, well, what's the use? I still feel God has let me down," I wailed. "Now I understand why people take their lives."

I reached for the car door handle and moved it, to express my feelings. Prince reached over as I unlatched the door. The car was going fast, and I was sorely tempted to end it right there. Thank the Lord I did not yield to the moment of weakness, but inwardly, I cried out to God for help, and slowly took my hand off the door handle. One moment the tears were flowing in contrition, and the next moment, I was striking out in frustration, and grief.

"Honey, is this our reward for serving God all our lives?" I cried.

Prince tried to console me, reminding me that there was a purpose in it all. "God is still in control. Honey, the story is not over yet. Remember, God hasn't forgotten or deserted us." In my heart, I knew the Lord had never forsaken us, but the enemy of our souls plotted and labored to blot out God's reality and closeness by using adverse circumstances.

In a broken voice, I wailed, "Why didn't somebody tell me?"

I was emotionally unable to continue talking and handed the phone to Prince, who graciously said goodbye for me. I flung myself across the bed, sobbing. I had never known such utter sorrow and grief, not even when my beloved father died. I had sensed peace in the family at the time of my father's decease. Now, with my brother Arden's death, everything was in a tragic state.

I struggled against intense emotions. I had been so certain that God would keep my brother alive until my family could be harmoniously reunited.

I was overwhelmed with the feeling that God had again let me down. Yet, down deep in my heart, I knew God had never let me down. I cried out to Him for mercy and help.

The air was electric as we sat in hushed, deathly silence, waiting for the verdict to be handed down from a pompous judge. Suddenly he started speaking in a slow, easy drawl.

Yesterday we felt he would be fair, honest, and favorable to the plaintiffs and their witnesses; he seemed concerned and understanding as he listened to the causes of action.

With a start, my mind came to attention. I did not like what I was hearing. The judge who was talking today did not sound like the man of previous days. My thoughts quickly became a battlefield of emotions. Immediately I wondered who had bought him off; what he was saying sounded so corrupt, I felt nauseated. I leaned over and whispered to my husband, Prince, sitting beside me, "I cannot stand it. I have to get out of here." I reached for my purse on his lap, where he had been using it for a writing table.

Instantly Prince whispered, "No, you are not. You sit still. That wouldn't be a good Christian testimony."

I struggled to get my purse, but my attempts were futile against his strong grasp. During that brief struggle, I glanced up to catch the unfriendly, judgmental eyes of the defense attorney watching us with interest. I settled back to listen.

A few moments later, I knew I could not listen any longer; this was the fourth day of a dreadful nightmare. I hastily snatched my jacket, leaving my purse behind, and quickly stood up and stepped around my husband. I marched across the courtroom to the exit, casting a final accusing glance at the betrayer—the pompous judge—only to find my efforts wasted; his eyes were averted.

I quickly closed the door behind me. The resounding bang echoed down the corridors of the stately old courthouse. I had not purposely slammed the door, but I made no effort to be quiet. Somehow, in my flight, I felt a little better hearing the echo of that door delivering my strong disapproval to everyone in the courtroom.

As I made my hasty departure, I had no idea where I was going. I only knew I had to get out of there to avoid an explosion of built-up emotions.

I descended the three flights of marble steps that somehow looked menacing to me. A breath of fresh air greeted me as I stepped outside. Pausing a moment before descending another flight of steps to the sidewalk, I glanced across the street and saw a Goodwill store; I made a hasty decision to go there for refuge.

During my descent to the sidewalk, I glanced at the store again, and it suddenly looked threatening. In my good clothes and dress shoes, I started marching across the courtyard and down the sidewalk. I was in a hurry, and I was angry. A hymn became my agonized prayer:

For a long time, I had lofty expectations and felt God was working out the details of the problem involving my family. During that time, I fasted and prayed and believed God would perform a miracle of grace and healing in the courtroom that I had so recently fled. Alas, the disappointment was too great when I saw no apparent visible evidence of His working power in bringing justice and healing to the people involved. Since I had withdrawn from the litigation, I thought God would reward me by intervening in an obvious way.

I was in a daze, oblivious to the cars and people around me, as I kept marching down Main Street, reliving previous days and episodes. My communion with God was concentrated as I walked along, talking with Him; I was walking the sidewalk in this world but walking in the Spirit in another. As I was hurrying along my heart was crying out to God to receive His grace and help. The awesome presence of the Lord was so very real to me during this time of deep sorrow and anguish of spirit.

After reading the above preface, Mr. Edwards asked, "May we

kneel around your manuscript and lay hands on it and pray God's blessing over it and your lives?"

I gave my consent and watched as the men, with my husband, knelt around the manuscript and earnestly prayed God's richest blessing on the book and on our lives. Those men had a rich prison ministry, helping the men behind iron bars, and they knew how to respond to the Lord and minister to the needs of hurting individuals. Praise God for their faithfulness.

I had no idea of the testing that was ahead of us. Prince and I thank God for the beautiful relationship we have maintained with each other and with our children through all of this. Without God's help and our deep love for each other, we never would have survived an ordeal of this kind that continued for years.

Sometimes it seemed a nightmare, only we did not wake up and find it gone. Those six years of testing made life's previous problems seem as nothing by comparison.

Shortly, I (Princess) came out of my deep meditation, only to realize I was not dreaming but in the real world.

My steps quickened as my mind continued on a battlefield of emotions. Often David's prayers became my prayers. Psalm 56 aptly described the emotions that kept tumbling over within me.

> Be merciful unto me, O God:
> for man would swallow me up;
> he fighting daily oppresseth me.
> Mine enemies would daily swallow
> me up: for they be many that
> fight against me, O thou most High.
> What time I am afraid, I will trust
> in thee. (Psalm 56:1–3)

> But now, O Lord, thou art our
> father: we are the clay, and thou
> our potter: and we all are the work
> of thy hand. (Isaiah 64:8)

Prince described the tests of life that were hurled at us so well:

"It is said that one picture is worth a thousand words; we hope that a word picture will portray some of our feelings and emotions in the crucible of testing. On various occasions, I have watched the breakers dash against the rocks and beaches of the Pacific Ocean. During our 'hour of proving,' I felt as though the breakers of divine dealing were pulverizing me. One wave would hurl me to the beach, crushing me beneath its weight and fury; then, while attempting to rise and escape the oncoming breaker, I was hit again and buried beneath the relentless force. It happened repeatedly, until strength was gone, and I would lie on the bosom of God, broken, silent, pliable, and listen to His voice.

"Yes, we have known both the 'severity' and the 'goodness' of God, yet our confession remains: 'He hath done all things well.'

"Through sharing some of God's dealings in our lives, we sincerely pray that others may be helped. No man is an island; each one touches another; we help or hinder, bless or curse. We have no ax to grind; we only want to bless and help other pilgrims on their journey through life. To God be the glory!"

After reading the above preface, Mr. Edwards asked, "May we kneel around your manuscript and lay hands on it and pray God's blessing over it and your lives?"

I gave my consent, and watched as the men, with my husband, knelt around the manuscript and earnestly prayed God's richest blessing on the book and on our lives. Those men had a rich prison ministry, helping the men behind iron bars, and they knew how to respond to the Lord and minister to the needs of hurting individuals. Praise God for their faithfulness.

I had no idea of the testing that was ahead of us. Prince and I thank God for the beautiful relationship we have maintained with each other, and with our children through all of this. Without God's help, and our deep love for each other, we never would have survived an ordeal of this kind that continued for years.

Sometimes it seemed a nightmare, only we did not wake up and find it gone. Those six years of testing made life's previous problems seem as nothing by comparison.

A divine principle prevails. Victory in one test only prepares us for future assignments, which are more difficult. This is the way it is in school—when the students pass one test they go on to higher, more difficult tests.

Shortly, I (Princess) came out of my deep meditation, only to realize I was not dreaming but in the real world.

My steps quickened as my mind continued on a battlefield of emotions. Often David's prayers became my prayers. Psalm 56 aptly described the emotions that kept tumbling over within me.

I continued in my flight down the street, as if marching to the beat of a drum—block after block until they stretched into miles; people and cars passed by in a blur. I marched on, determined to put distance between that detestable courtroom and me.

A famous college campus came into view with its beautiful, lush green lawns. I could not resist the attraction of a quiet, peaceful-looking stream in the middle of the campus and on impulse stepped across the grass to a small bridge overlooking the gentle-flowing creek.

I stood for some time gazing down into the cool, refreshing water. How wonderful it would be if life would flow like that—calm and peaceful. I leaned over to rest my elbows on the bridge railing and hid my face in my hands, as tears spilled into the water where they mingled and became one with the quiet/tranquil stream below. I felt ashamed that my precious family had been reduced to a courtroom battle among themselves. How could such a thing be possible?

In agony, I cried softly to God. "Why, oh, why? What does it all mean? My dear family ensnared in one of Satan's devious plots. Please, God, help us. Please bring restoration, peace, and harmony to our loved ones again."

After communing with God in the peace and quiet of my surroundings, I felt panicky lest an unwelcome person should drive by and see me. I knew I must get back to the road and hurry on. Even though no one else knew where I was, it was wonderful to know Jesus was with me.

My feet were getting sore. I stopped to slip off my shoes, and while rubbing my feet, I discovered blisters on several toes; also, the balls of my feet were excruciatingly sore. Determined, I put my shoes back on and continued, but my steps were getting slower and slower. Finally, I wrapped a handkerchief around the sore toes on my left foot and with difficulty gently pressed it back into my dress sandal. It offered little relief, since some of the blisters had already broken, and the bottoms of my feet were crying for mercy. I was tempted to sit down or lie down by the roadside and nurse my wounds, but I gritted my teeth and hurried on.

> For he shall give his angels
> charge over thee, to keep thee
> in all thy ways. They shall bear
> thee up in their hands, lest thou
> dash thy foot against a stone. (Psalm 91:11–12)

I was sure God felt sorry for me as I cried to Him for help. I looked up in time to see a familiar car coming toward me; it made a sweeping turn in the road directly in front of me. The passenger door was flung open, and I willingly climbed in. Words were unnecessary as I read the pain in my husband's eyes. In response, I began to sob; we silently communed with each other, each sensing the love and caring of the other. It is beautiful how a husband and wife can do that.

I had been selfish in my anger, not thinking of my husband and his concern for me, especially when he could not find me in the courthouse. His concern grew and was enhanced by his knowledge of my poor sense of direction; he knew that I could easily get lost. Prince realized that I was emotionally upset, feeling forsaken by my mother and betrayed by some members of my family. He told me that he prayed God would take care of me, keep me from harm, and help him find me. The stress was mirrored on his face.

During my flight, I had longed for a wheat field to hide in, as I had one time in my childhood. I remembered hiding among the grain stalks to quiet myself and nurse my wounded feelings. There I found God's healing touch, but this time there was no grain field for refuge. Now I had my caring husband arriving in time to care for me.

"Thank you, Jesus, for your loving concern; I know I can find safety in your faithful loving care. And you said you would never leave us nor forsake us."

> The Lord is my light and my salvation; whom shall
> I fear? The Lord is the strength of my life; of whom
> shall I be afraid? (Psalm 27:1)

One of Albert's gospel messages:

Bitter or Better

Scripture: "Let all bitterness, and wrath, and anger, and clamour, and evil speaking, be put away from you, with all malice: And be ye kind one to another, tenderhearted, forgiving one another, even as God for Christ's sake hath forgiven you" (Ephesians 4:31–32).

Introduction: Sooner or later *bad* things—hurts, disappointments, wrongs done to us—happen to everyone. No one is immune. To suffer because of our own foolishness, because we made a bad decision, because of our own sin, in one sense is to be expected; but to suffer because of someone else's wrongdoing is quite another. However, we need to remember, when we suffer because of another's sin, we still are free to make a personal decision. Will I become *bitter* or will I choose to become *better*? No one else can make that decision for us; we must do it ourselves. Consider real people in God's Word who had to make this decision.

1. Joseph:

A. Genesis 37–50

1. Hated by his older brothers.
2. Sold into slavery by those same brothers.
3. Potiphar's wife endeavored to seduce him; because of his staying true to God and being lied about by Potiphar's wife, he was thrown into prison.
4. In prison, he became a faithful slave/servant.
5. Joseph simply kept on serving God where he was and all without *bitterness*.
6. His faithfulness to God—without the bondage of bitterness, caused him to be elevated in responsibility and ultimately

became the means of saving his own family from starvation. In short, he became a *better* person!

2. Apostle Paul:

A. "Are they ministers of Christ? (I speak as a fool) I am more; in labours more abundant, in stripes above measure, in prisons more frequent, in deaths oft. Of the Jews five times received I forty stripes save one. Thrice was I beaten with rods, once was I stoned, thrice I suffered shipwreck, a night and a day I have been in the deep; In journeyings often, in perils of waters, in perils of robbers, in perils by mine own countrymen, in perils by the heathen, in perils in the city, in perils in the wilderness, in perils in the sea, in perils among false brethren, in weariness and painfulness, in watchings often, in hunger and thirst, in fastings often, in cold and nakedness. Beside those things that are without, that which cometh upon me daily, the care of all the churches" (2 Corinthians 11:23–28).

1. Yet despite all these hardships, Paul kept a sweet spirit and wrote a major part of the New Testament.
2. You will find no trace of *bitterness* in the attitude and spirit of Apostle Paul.
3. He became *better.*
4. "For I determined not to know anything among you, save Jesus Christ, and him crucified" (1 Corinthians 2:2).

3. John, the Beloved:

A. Exiled on the Isle of Patmos for the testimony of Jesus Christ.

1. Though separated from family and friends, God gave him visions and revelations concerning end-time events—things that will be fulfilled perhaps in our lifetime.
2. You will find no bitterness in the attitude and spirit of John— only a willingness to be used of God. Thus, he became better!

IV. Conclusion: No one can control all the circumstances and events that come to us day by day. Oftentimes things happen over which we have no control. However, each one of us *can* control our *reaction* to what transpires in our lives. We can make a conscious choice whether we will allow the events of our lives to make us *bitter* or *better*. We can become bitter as acid—mean, sour, miserable to be with or near—or we can use (with God's grace and help) the happenings of our lives to make us more loving, kind, and considerate of others—more like Jesus! Consider Jesus: "He is despised and rejected of men; a man of sorrows, and acquainted with grief: and we hid as it were our faces from him; he was despised and we esteemed him not. Surely he hath borne our griefs, and carried our sorrows: yet we did esteem him stricken, smitten of God, and afflicted. But he was wounded for our transgressions, he was bruised for our iniquities: the chastisement of our peace was upon him; and with his stripes we are healed. All we like sheep have gone astray; we have turned everyone to his own way; and the Lord hath laid upon him the iniquity of us all" (Isaiah 53:3–6).

> I will praise thee, O Lord, among the people: and I will sing praises unto thee among the nations.
>
> For thy mercy is great above the heavens: and thy truth reacheth unto the clouds.
>
> Be thou exalted, O God, above the heavens: and thy glory above all the earth. (Psalm 108:3–5)

ABOUT THE AUTHORS

Aimee Filan Anderson, daughter of Olaus and Minnie Filan, was born near Hay, Washington, in Whitman County and grew up on a wheat ranch. After high school graduation from Wa Hi in Walla Walla, Washington, she attended Northwest College in Kirkland, Washington.

On April 9, 1954, Aimee married Albert E. Anderson, an evangelist and minister in the Assemblies of God. Together they traveled throughout the United States while holding evangelistic meetings, until they accepted their first pastorate in 1957.

For fifty-nine years, lacking one month to the day (as of March 9, 2013), Aimee was a minister's wife. She has ministered as a Sunday school superintendent, church pianist, and a leader in church organizations. She also still is an ordained (The Fellowship) minister. Over the past years, Aimee helped her husband pastor ten churches throughout the state of Washington. While their six children, Deborah, Rebecca, Mary, Eunice, Mark, and Jonathan were still living at home, the Anderson family performed numerous musical concerts.

As of August 23, 2022, in addition to being blessed with four daughters and two sons, her family now includes four sons-in-law, one daughter-in-law, thirty-four grandchildren (including the ones who have married into our family), and twenty-eight great-grandchildren, which brings the total to seventy-three children, grandchildren, and great-grandchildren. Praise the Lord!

April 9, 2013, was Albert and Aimee's fifty-ninth anniversary, which they missed celebrating together on this earth by only one month to the day. All praise be to God for all those wonderful years of love and companionship!

Aimee has authored and/or coauthored nine books and coproduced one movie, *A Murder of Innocence* (2018), based on her first book, *Broken, Yet Triumphant.*

https://amurderofinnocencemovie.com

Aimee authored her first book, *Broken, Yet Triumphant,* in **1983**. It is a memoir, based upon her true-life story. The movie, *A Murder of Innocence* (trailer and personal Interview with Aimee), was produced in (2018), based on Aimee's first book, *Broken, Yet Triumphant.*

Sunshine through Clouds, in 2001, is the sequel to her first book; her deceased husband became the coauthor. A courtroom and familial drama—the way of justice and forgiveness—is not always an easy path followed.

Albert and Aimee then coauthored a series of four books on the corruption that is often present within the church leadership and US government. It is nothing but the candid truth of illegal activities that occurred in churches from the very people who often preach about following God's laws. The corruption revealed in the church leadership years ago is still prevalent today in the church leadership, US government, and political world.

The first of the Exposed book series was *Whited Sepulchres,* in 1996, followed by its sequel, *A Generation of Vipers,* in 2001. Thereafter, its sequel, *White Collar Crime in the Church,* in 2004, and its sequel, *Grand Jury Mystery,* in 2008.

Aimee and Albert coauthored their fascinating love story, action-filled storybook (their memoir), based on some of their true-life experiences, *Our Awesome Journey,* in **2014**. Aimee finished this book and published it after her dear husband, Albert, was called to his heavenly home. Aimee then authored, *A Legacy of Love Letters,* in 2019. Followed by *I Have Kept the Faith,* in 2021. And this book, Silenced: Refused to be Silenced, in 2023.

Personal Life Series
Broken, Yet Triumphant

A Legacy of Love Letters
Author: Aimee Filan Anderson

Sunshine through Clouds
Author: Aimee Filan Anderson
Coauthor: Albert E. Anderson

Our Awesome Journey

I Have Kept the Faith
Authors: Albert and Aimee Anderson

Church Investigation Series

Whited Sepulchres
A Generation of Vipers
White-Collar Crime in the Church
Grand Jury Mystery
Silenced: Refused to Be Silenced
Authors: Albert and Aimee Anderson

Movie

A Murder of Innocence

Based on Aimee Filan Anderson's first book,
Broken, Yet Triumphant

Coproducers:
Aimee Filan Anderson and Shawn Justice

The feature-length drama film *A Murder of Innocence* follows Aimee, her pastor husband, Albert, and their six children—Deborah, Rebecca, Mary, Eunice, Mark, and Jonathan—as they discover through terrible tragedy that "faith in the night as well as the day," "praying without ceasing," and "praising the Lord, throughout the day and night," brings the "wonderful peace of God" that floods our hearts and lives.

God gave Albert and Aimee grace and strength to endure the test of faith! Praise the Lord! God enabled them to "love their enemies" and keep their hearts full of love for the wounded and bleeding. They still loved the Lord; God means everything to them. They made a choice to become better instead of bitter, no matter what the trial and test of their faith that they had to endure. This tragic story needed to be told by way of the pen. And now may a new (second) movie follow this book, in a very productive, interesting, exciting, informative, revealing, and very dramatic way—while at the same time bring glory and honor to our wonderful Lord Jesus Christ, and Savior and Lord, God Almighty, our wonderful Heavenly Father! *"Praise the Lord." "Thank you, Jesus."*

Printed in the United States
by Baker & Taylor Publisher Services